The world is in peril.

An ancient evil is rising from beneath Erdas, and we need YOU to help stop it.

Claim your spirit animal and join the adventure now:

1. Go to scholastic.com/spiritanimals.

2. Log in to create your character and choose your own spirit animal.

3. Have your book ready and enter the code below to unlock the adventure.

Your code: NNHXWHNX2X

By the Four Fallen,
The Greencloaks

We are all
of Erdas, united.

HEART OF THE LAND

Sarah Prineas

SCHOLASTIC INC.

To all the Greencloak readers and
your spirit animal companions. —S.P.

This book is a work of fiction. Names, characters, places, and
incidents are either the product of the author's imagination or are used
fictitiously, and any resemblance to actual persons, living or dead, business
establishments, events, or locales is entirely coincidental.

Library of Congress Control Number: 2016962660

ISBN 978-1-338-11665-6

10 9 8 7 6 5 4 3 2 1   17 18 19 20 21

Book design by Charice Silverman
First edition, May 2017

Printed in the U.S.A. 23

Scholastic US: 557 Broadway • New York, NY 10012
Scholastic Canada: 604 King Street West • Toronto, ON M5V 1E1
Scholastic New Zealand Limited: Private Bag 94407 • Greenmount, Manukau 2141
Scholastic UK Ltd.: Euston House • 24 Eversholt Street • London NW1 1DB

HEART OF THE LAND

1

PRINCESS SONG

PRINCESS SONG, DAUGHTER OF THE EMPEROR OF ZHONG, paced her chamber in the Council Citadel. Soon the leaders of the four main governments of Erdas, plus Stetriol, would meet for the first time since they'd gone into hiding during the turmoils of the Devourer's invasions and the Wyrm's attack.

A certain princess had not been invited to this meeting.

She was not happy about it.

Song remembered to make her steps small and dainty, not the sweeping strides she felt like taking. From the outside, she knew she looked serene, her black hair braided and held in place with jewel-tipped pins, her robe exquisitely embroidered in the colors of deep ocean green and rich emerald. Inside, her heart fluttered. She wanted to be more than decorative. She was determined to be a princess in deed and not just in name.

From the hallway came the sound of heavy footsteps, a guard speaking, and then the heavy door of Song's chamber swung open. The Emperor of Zhong entered, followed by two of his Oathbound guards, both wearing

1

plain black uniforms with brass wrist protectors and brass neck-collars that kept their chins held high. The blank-faced Oathbound took up their stations on either side of the door.

The emperor was a big man dressed in ceremonial armor made of lacquered and gilded bamboo. It clattered when he walked. He wore his hair long in a warrior's braid, even though, Song knew, he hadn't fought in the war against the Devourer. He had been in hiding, guarded by his loyal Oathbound, just as the Queen of Eura, the Prime Minister of Amaya, and the High Chieftain of Nilo had been. Now that the danger had passed, they all had taken up their old positions again, ruling the world.

"Daughter," the emperor said in a deep, commanding voice.

Song lowered her eyes, folded her hands gracefully together, and bowed low, showing deep respect. "Father," she said softly.

As she straightened, her father's sharp eyes studied her, looking for any fault, any blemish. Song held herself still under his gaze. His eyes narrowed as he saw the emerald and ocean of her embroidered robe—green was not a favored color at the moment. "I understand you wished to speak with me," he said.

Song bowed again. "Yes, honored Father. With your permission, I would like to attend the meeting of the Council tomorrow."

"The meeting is for the leaders of Erdas," he responded.

Song clenched her hands together, then forced herself to relax. She couldn't let him see how much this meant to her. "Please, Father," she begged.

The emperor observed her again for a long, judging moment. His mouth settled into a strict line, and Song knew what his answer would be before he spoke. "No," he said. No further explanation, no justification.

"But–" Song blurted.

Her father raised a hand, silencing her. "The meeting is no place for a dutiful daughter."

"I will not speak," Song promised. "I will only be an observer."

His face stayed as still as if it had been carved out of jade. Song knew that look. He was angry.

"It will be good," she said quietly, "if the other leaders of Erdas can see that your daughter survived the recent conflicts. Thanks to your care and foresight." She glanced quickly at the guards who flanked the door. "And the loyalty of the Oathbound."

The straight line of his mouth relaxed. Slowly the emperor nodded. "Very well. But you will remain silent and standing behind my chair." His gaze flicked over her again. "And you will wear a robe of a more suitable color."

Song lowered her eyes so he would not see the sudden wave of fury that had risen in her. Always he treated her this way, as if she were an object–a beautiful doll– but not his living, breathing daughter. Carefully she bowed. "It will be as you say, Father."

As the emperor turned and left the room, Song held her bow until she heard the Oathbound guards close the door behind him. Then she straightened. If she could have seen her face in a mirror, she would have noticed that her mouth was set in the same straight line as her father's.

She would attend the meeting, but not as mere observer. She would not stay silent. The Council–and her father–would hear what she had to say.

THE CITADEL

"**I** DON'T LIKE THE LOOK OF THIS PLACE," ROLLAN SAID, gazing up at the Council Citadel. It was a massive castle built of dark-gray stone, quarried from the Petral Mountains, which loomed behind it like a bank of storm clouds.

From the road where she stood with Rollan, Meilin, and Conor, Abeke could see that the Citadel consisted of a huge central tower; jutting out from it were four "wings," each built in the style of one of the four main lands of Erdas. The brightly colored flags of Nilo, Zhong, Eura, and Amaya hung from a wide gateway in the main tower, but they couldn't hide the fact that half the Citadel's windows were broken. Moss encrusted the slate roofs, and several of the walls looked ready to buckle under their own weight.

To Abeke, the Citadel looked like what it was: an important building that had been neglected for a long time.

Meilin's nose wrinkled. "It is a little run-down, isn't it?" She stood next to Rollan. Jhi was a furry black-and-white boulder at Meilin's other side.

"More than a little," Abeke said. She pointed at the part of the Citadel that had been built in the blocky style of a Niloan fortress. "Do you see the holes in the roof there? If it rains, anybody sleeping in those rooms will wake up in a wet bed." She glanced over her shoulder at Conor, who stood half a pace behind the other three.

Abeke waited for him to add something, to make a comment about the Council Citadel. But he did not speak. The fight against the Wyrm had ended months ago, but it was clear to her that Conor was still gripped by the horror of what the Wyrm's parasite had done to him. The Wyrm had affected many of the Greencloaks. She and Uraza had been marked by it, too, but somehow it had been worse for Conor. At least he had the strong, steadfast support of Briggan, who never left his side.

Just as she had Uraza. Abeke felt the leopard sitting close beside her—closer than usual, trying to reassure her that their bond held, after it had been so cruelly ripped apart by Zerif. Uraza's ears were pricked, and her long, fluffy tail curled around Abeke's ankles. Abeke smiled at Conor, trying to get a smile from him in response.

Conor looked away, rubbing his forehead as if it ached. *Maybe it does*, Abeke thought. The Wyrm's hideous black spiral had pulsed on Conor's brow for many days. The mark was faded now, but Abeke knew better than any of them that the horrors of the Wyrm could not be easily forgotten. If Conor needed her, she vowed to herself, she would be there for him.

"We'd better go inside," Meilin said. "We don't want to be late."

"We already are late," Rollan added. Overhead, Essix flew in a wide circle, a distant shape against a cloudy gray sky.

"Olvan and Lenori and the rest of the Greencloak contingent must be here already," Abeke said.

"And we would've been on time," Rollan put in, "if a certain black-and-white bear hadn't stuffed herself with an entire forest of bamboo and then needed three days to recover."

"It's not Jhi's fault her favorite food just happened to be growing beside that inn," Meilin protested.

When they'd received the summons from Olvan, Meilin and Rollan had been traveling together to see Jano Rion, the city where Meilin had grown up. Conor, Abeke knew, had been with his family near Trunswick. She hoped they had taken good care of him, but she knew the simple shepherds couldn't really understand everything that had happened to him. After re-bonding with Uraza in Stetriol, Abeke had gone to see Kirat and Cabaro in Nilo.

She had missed her friends, but it had been good to have a rest—and to go out with Uraza and her bow and a quiver of obsidian-tipped arrows, hunting for gazelle. She and Uraza had been about to travel farther south to visit her family in Okaihee when the summons had arrived. As eager as she'd been to see her friends again, she had enjoyed a little time without the excitement and worry that came with being a Greencloak. And not just any Greencloak—one of the Four Heroes of Erdas.

Obeying Olvan's summons, the four of them had met up at Greenhaven, but they had arrived too late to travel with the rest of the Greencloaks. After hurrying to cross Eura, they had taken a coach that left them a mile down the road from their destination, to give their animals some time to stretch their legs (or wings, in Essix's case) before they were cooped up in the Citadel.

The Four Heroes of Erdas, along with Briggan, Jhi, Uraza, and Essix overhead, headed for the Citadel's main gate, a stone arch with a raised portcullis that looked like a row of iron teeth. The flags of the four lands fluttered in the breeze.

"No Greencloak flag," Meilin observed.

Abeke wasn't sure what to think of that.

Five guards dressed all in black, armored with brass vambraces and collars, watched as the four kids approached. All the guards wore swords sheathed at their hips, but only one of them was Marked, a big woman with pale blond hair cut very short. Around her upper arm was coiled a slim brown snake. As the leader of the guards, she held up a hand, stopping them. The snake twined down her arm and threaded itself through her fingers. Its tongue flickered, tasting the air.

Conor stepped up beside Abeke. "I know that kind of snake," he whispered to her. "It's from Eura, a stone viper."

"Is it dangerous?" Abeke asked.

Conor nodded. "It's not often seen. It hides under rocks, but its bite is deadly poisonous. Its venom turns its victims into stone, and they can only be saved by an antidote."

"Halt," ordered the Marked woman. "I'm Brunhild the Merry." The woman's already sour face deepened into a frown. Abeke wondered if perhaps "merry" was a family name. This person certainly didn't look very happy to see them. "I demand that you state your business," Brunhild barked.

Meilin pointed at her green cloak, then at Jhi. "These make our business pretty obvious, don't you think? We're here as part of the Greencloak contingent."

"The Greencloaks arrived yesterday," the woman named Brunhild said. Her voice sounded slithery, almost like a snake's. "They didn't say anything about a bunch of kids joining them. This is a gathering of the leaders of Erdas. You have no standing here."

"Excuse me?" Rollan said, folding his arms. "We're not just *a bunch of kids*. We saved the world."

"Twice," Abeke said.

"Heroes of Erdas," Rollan added. "Maybe you've heard of us?"

"You think I've heard of four sniveling brats?" the guard sneered.

"*I'm* not a brat," Rollan said. He glanced aside at Abeke. "Are you a brat?"

"No," Abeke answered. "And I don't snivel, either." She had a bad feeling about this. Clearly Uraza did, too; she felt the leopard grow tense, ready to pounce. She laid a hand on her spirit animal's head, steadying her.

Meilin sighed loudly. "Enough. We don't want a fight." Jhi lumbered to her side and sat, as immovable as a wall. "The Greencloak leader, Olvan, summoned us. Whether he left word about us or not, we're supposed to be here."

"I don't think so," snapped Brunhild the Merry. She put a hand to her sword and took a swaggering step forward. "You may not enter. Now leave here, *Greencloaks*." She hissed the last word as if it were a curse.

Beside Conor, Briggan emitted a low, rumbling growl. The thick ruff of fur at his neck bristled.

In response, the guard held out her hand; the snake that was coiled around her wrist reared back as if ready to strike. Abeke saw the glint of poison dripping from its retractable fangs.

Conor's hand was on his ax. Meilin drew her own sword and took up a fighting stance. Abeke fixed her eyes on the snake, ready to use her bow to block its strike if it came for any of them.

"Don't let them enter the Citadel!" Brunhild the Merry ordered. The other four guards surged forward, drawing their swords.

"No blood!" Meilin warned as Abeke nocked an arrow. Abeke nodded, understanding. They were not going to gain entrance to the Citadel by wounding or killing its guards. They *had* been invited; they shouldn't have to invade!

With a yell, one of the guards chopped a sword at Meilin, who coolly sidestepped it and nodded for Briggan and Conor to deal with him. Three more guards converged on her. Abeke saw Meilin smile slightly, and then suddenly she laughed and tossed her sword straight up into the air. As it spun upward, flashing in the light, Meilin elbowed one of the charging guards in the head, whirled to duck a sword thrust and swept the legs from a second guard, and then, as her sword reached the top of its arc and began to fall, she used a palm-strike to the chest to take out the third guard. The sword fell. As it reached her, Meilin snatched it out of the air by the hilt and waved its point threateningly over the three guards who writhed in pain at her feet.

Meanwhile Briggan had his powerful jaws clenched around the leg of a fourth guard—not enough to draw blood, but enough to make her screech and try to wriggle away. And Uraza had flattened Brunhild the Merry with one leap. The leopard had her front paws on the woman's chest, so she couldn't get up. Brunhild's stone viper was nowhere to be seen.

Abeke wanted to laugh. The entire fight had taken less than ten seconds, and she hadn't had to fire a single arrow.

"Look out!" she heard Rollan shout, and turned to see ten more black-clad figures armed with swords and spears pour out of a guard house next to the Citadel gate.

Uraza snarled, and Abeke drew back her bowstring. There *was* going to be blood after all.

Abeke was about to let an arrow fly when she heard a high voice call, "Stop!" She saw a swirl of green silk as a black-haired girl strode from the gateway and stepped between the Citadel guards and the four Greencloaks and their spirit animals. She was tiny, no taller than a ten-year-old child, but her face was very beautiful and she looked their own age, or maybe a little older. When she spoke, her voice was commanding. "Stand down," she ordered the guards. To Abeke's astonishment, they immediately sheathed their swords and grounded their spears. The guards the Greencloaks had defeated scrambled away, picking up the weapons they'd dropped during the fight.

Brunhild the Merry climbed to her feet, then stepped back and bowed her head. There was still no sign of her stone viper. "Your Highness," she murmured.

The girl nodded briskly, then turned to face the four Greencloaks. For a moment Abeke caught a glimpse of something in the girl's face besides beauty—power, maybe, and determination or anger—and then whatever it was became hidden as the girl placed her tiny feet together, primly folded her hands, and nodded gracefully.

"I, Princess Song, daughter of the Emperor of Zhong, welcome you. I beg you to forgive these guards. They are

Oathbound, and thus are sworn to protect the leaders of the four lands, and so they acted hastily, seeking to bar you from the Citadel."

Abeke lowered her bow. She, Conor, and Rollan all looked at Meilin, hoping she would respond. Not because she was from Zhong, like Princess Song, but because she had been trained in etiquette and knew best what to say in situations like this.

Meilin straightened and sheathed her sword. Looking every inch the daughter of a high-ranking Zhongese general, she nodded to the princess. "They did act too fast. As you saw, we had no trouble with the first five guards. We could have easily taken the rest of them, too."

Abeke heard Brunhild the Merry give a derisive snort.

"It may be so," Princess Song said. She turned a frowning gaze on the guards. "These are the Heroes of Erdas," she explained to them. "They are the young Greencloaks who so bravely fought the Devourer and helped save us all from the Wyrm. Brunhild, you and the other Oathbound were in hiding with the leaders, so you did not witness their acts of bravery. You should do these young people honor."

Reluctantly the Oathbound guards bowed.

"Now," Princess Song added, "I will bring the young Greencloaks to their chambers." She turned to lead the way into the Citadel.

But before they could follow, Brunhild raised her hand, stopped them. "A moment, Your Highness," she interrupted. "Perhaps you forget the rules of this place." Her mouth stretched into an ugly, particularly un-merry smile. "The Greencloaks cannot bring their spirit animals inside."

"What?" Abeke asked, not understanding. They couldn't exactly leave their spirit animals outside, while they went in.

Brunhild folded her brawny arms across her chest; her snake, which had remained hidden during the fight, slithered onto her shoulder, where it rested its slim head, watching them with slitted red eyes. "To be admitted to the Citadel, you Greencloaks must put your animals into their passive states."

"Yours isn't," Meilin argued.

"Because I am a loyal Oathbound, a protector of the leaders of Erdas," Brunhild said smugly. "*You* are Greencloaks. Clearly not to be trusted, since you attacked us just now without provocation."

That was an outright *lie*! The Oathbound had attacked them first. Abeke opened her mouth to protest, but fell silent when Meilin shook her head and drew the three of them aside for a quiet word. "I hate to say this," Meilin whispered as they put their heads together, "but they're not entirely wrong."

"No, they're only completely wrong," Rollan put in, his voice low and angry.

"Yes, Brunhild was lying about us attacking the guards," Meilin said, "but they do have a reason not to trust us."

Abeke saw Conor reach up to rub his forehead, where the mark of the Wyrm had been, and she knew what this meant.

"Oh," Abeke breathed. "It's because so many of the Greencloaks were taken by the parasites and forced to serve the Wyrm."

Meilin nodded reluctantly. "A lot happened when Zerif had his own little personal army of Greencloaks. We may be mistrusted by some people who don't know the full story." She cast an apologetic glance at Conor, who wouldn't meet her eyes. "I think we'll have to do as they say."

"I don't like it," Rollan said flatly. As if responding to his anger, Essix dove, swooped low over their heads, then arced back into the cloudy sky.

"I don't like it, either," Meilin shot back. "But I don't think we have any choice."

Slowly, the four of them straightened. Meilin reached up to ruffle the black fur behind Jhi's ears. Without speaking, she held out her arm. She would never *order* the panda to take the passive state, not after their history together, but she would hope for the best. Jhi sighed deeply and then disappeared, reappearing as a black-and-white tattoo on Meilin's forearm. "As you see," Meilin said to Princess Song and the Oathbound guards. "We will abide by the Citadel rules."

"You do us great honor," Princess Song said softly.

Conor had already called Briggan into the passive state. Seeing as she had no choice, Abeke stroked a finger over the fine fur of Uraza's nose and then gave the leopard a nod. Uraza disappeared with a flash.

Rollan stood with his hands on his hips, gazing up at the sky. His green cloak was more ragged and faded than the newer cloaks the rest of them wore. It fluttered in the breeze. Essix circled high above, riding that breeze, showing no sign of descending again.

"Well?" Meilin asked him.

"She has no intention of coming down here," Rollan said, not taking his eyes from the bird.

Meilin rolled her eyes, then nodded at Abeke and Conor. "You two had better go in and get settled. We'll wait out here until Essix is feeling more cooperative."

"It could be a while," Rollan put in.

"Then it's a good thing I'm so patient," Meilin replied.

"*You*, patient?" Abeke heard Rollan say, and then Meilin said something in response that made him laugh.

Abeke followed Princess Song and Brunhild through the huge gate of the Citadel; Conor trailed behind her, looking around with wide eyes. The flags of the four regions flapped overhead, and the sharp iron teeth of the portcullis seemed about to take a bite of them. Abeke shivered, already missing the reassurance of having Uraza at her side, and hurried to keep up. The princess was tiny, but she walked swiftly, sweepingly, as she led them up a set of broad stairs to the main double doors of the Citadel's central chamber.

"You are Abeke, are you not?" Princess Song asked, falling into step beside her. At Abeke's nod, Song glanced back at Conor, who lingered behind them. "I hope you can answer my question. I have heard that one of you—Conor—was taken by the Wyrm. Is this so?"

Abeke glanced quickly back. Conor's face was blank, but he was only a step behind; he must have heard the princess's question.

"By one of the Wyrm's parasites," Abeke corrected.

"I'm sorry to have to ask this," Princess Song went on, "but he served your enemy. Are you certain that you can trust him?"

Abeke raised her voice, to be sure Conor would hear her next words. "He served the Wyrm against his will, and he is free of it now. He is just as trustworthy as the rest of us."

"That's not saying much," blond Brunhild put in, casting a suspicious glare over Conor.

Abeke felt her temper rise at the guard's remark, but she took a deep breath to calm herself. They'd had one fight at the gate; she couldn't start another one already.

They entered a huge entrance hall hung with curtains of cobwebs and dust. Princess Song flagged down a passing man dressed in plain brown. "This servant will direct Conor to his rooms in the Euran part of the Citadel, and I will bring you to your rooms in the Niloan wing, Abeke."

The brown-clad servant bowed and gestured toward a passage leading away. Conor started toward him.

"Wait," Abeke said abruptly, and Conor paused, looking over his shoulder at her with raised eyebrows. "Do you have separate rooms for all four of us?" she asked the princess.

"Of course," Song answered. "There is a place for Rollan in the Amayan wing, and I've requested that Meilin be given rooms next to mine in the Zhongese wing."

Abeke shook her head. Conor seemed all right to her at the moment, but he shouldn't be left alone. With Briggan forced into the passive state, Conor needed his friends around him. So did she, for that matter. "We will share a room," she said firmly.

Princess Song blinked. "All four of you?"

Conor rejoined them. "Yes," he said, nodding. "That would be good."

The big Oathbound guard was standing behind Princess Song. "I know of a good room for them, Your Highness," Brunhild said smoothly. She set off toward another hallway. Abeke, Princess Song, and Conor followed. "Though a prison cell might be the best place for the likes of you Greencloaks," Abeke heard Brunhild add under her breath.

Abeke came to a sudden stop. Conor crashed into her from behind, but she kept her feet. The Oathbound guard and Princess Song turned to face her.

"I am not one to make threats," Abeke said quietly. She felt Conor's warmth behind her; his presence gave her words weight and strength. "So listen well, Oathbound," she went on. "We are not called the Heroes of Erdas because we spent the Second Devourer War or the struggle against the Wyrm hiding in a bunker. We have fought, and we have lost much, and some of us have suffered in ways you can't even imagine. You will not say bad things about Conor, or any of the Greencloaks, or you will have me to answer to. Do you understand?"

Brunhild went pasty pale and fell back a step. Her stone viper was nowhere to be seen. "Y-yes," she stammered. "I understand."

Beside her, Princess Song raised a finely etched eyebrow. "Clearly, Abeke, you are fierce, just like your leopard spirit animal." She turned to face the guard, frowning. "These are honorable Greencloaks, Brunhild. Treat them as they deserve. Do you understand?"

Cringing, Brunhild bowed deeply. "Yes, Your Highness."

Princess Song gave Abeke and Conor an apologetic look. "I beg your forgiveness, young heroes. The Oathbound mean well. There's been so much destruction and confusion in the last year. And after so long serving as guards, they long to act."

"It's all right," Abeke said. On the one hand, Meilin had been right—the Greencloaks didn't have the best reputation at the moment, so the Oathbound couldn't be faulted for their bad attitudes. On the other hand, she thought the Oathbound could bear watching. They might be loyal guards, but it was possible that they could be dangerous, too. And clearly Brunhild did not live up to her name.

A MESSAGE

W HEN HE'D FIRST JOINED THE GREENCLOAKS, CONOR'S dreams had been powerful, prophetic. On their very first mission, he'd had a dream so vivid it had felt like real life—he had dreamed about Arax the Ram and the path to find him. Later, it had been his dream that had sent the Greencloaks to Stetriol for the final battle against Gerathon and the Conquerors, a vision that had led them to victory.

Now, every time he closed his eyes, his dreams were filled with black tendrils that reached out and pulled him into a sea of oozing slime. He struggled against the writhing tentacles, but they gripped him firmly, thrusting him toward four red eyes that arose from the darkness and glared malevolently at him. Then a huge, leechlike mouth appeared and gaped wide, revealing rows of triangular teeth dripping with corrosive acid.

The Wyrm!

Its grating shriek filled his head. The spiral mark on his brow amplified the sound until it was everywhere; there were no more Greencloaks, no more friendship or hope or light, no more Conor. He was the Wyrm and the Wyrm was him, and that was all.

The maw of the Wyrm gaped wider. The tendrils dragged him closer.

No! he shouted in his dream, struggling.

"No!"

And then he felt a hand on his arm, and he fought his way out of the oily darkness, opening his eyes to see someone gazing down at him, her brown eyes soft and worried.

Abeke. It was Abeke.

He took a ragged breath that was almost a sob.

"It's all right," she said quietly. She was on her knees next to the low bed. He remembered where they were. The room they'd been given was tiny, with one rickety bed, blank stone walls, a narrow slit of a window, and an inch of dust covering everything. In the distance was the sound of hammering–the Citadel being fixed up after years of neglect. Despite the noise, Conor had been so tired after their journey from Greenhaven. He'd sat down on the low bed just for a moment. . . .

He swallowed, his throat dry and raw as if he'd been shouting.

Maybe he had been. "I must have fallen asleep," he croaked. Slowly he sat up, leaning his back against a stone wall. It was cold and clammy. A swirl of dust glinted in the dim light that shone through the narrow window.

Abeke shifted to sit next to him. "Another nightmare?"

Conor nodded.

"The Wyrm?" Abeke pressed.

"Yes," Conor admitted. He reached up to rub the lingering ache in his forehead.

Intercepting his hand, Abeke pushed up his shirt-sleeve, exposing the shape of Briggan in his passive state, a dark mark on his pale skin. Then she placed her own arm next to his, the mark of her leopard a swirling spotted shape on her warm brown skin. "We both suffered," Abeke said. "The Wyrm took Uraza from me, and it took you from yourself." She stroked a hand over her tattoo as if petting the leopard. "But we came through it. We survived. And we'll keep surviving. We defeat the Wyrm every day that we go on."

Conor stared down at the marks of Briggan and Uraza, side by side. Somehow seeing them together made him feel better, even without the comforting feel of Briggan's rough head under his hand. He thought about how Abeke must feel. Her bond with Uraza had been shattered. And . . .

"Do you still think about him?" he asked.

"About Shane?" Abeke asked. At Conor's nod, she went on. "Yes. I'm still not sure how I feel about him. It's complicated. He betrayed me—more than once. I fought a duel against him, and it was the angriest I've ever been in my entire life. But he died saving me when Zerif forced Uraza to attack." She shook her head sadly. "Shane was my first friend." She leaned closer and looked into Conor's eyes. He saw wisdom in her face, and hope. "But you are my truest friend."

Conor wasn't sure what to say. As someone who had worn the Wyrm's mark on his forehead, did he deserve a friend like Abeke? He was saved from having to respond when the door banged open and Meilin and Rollan strode into the room.

And stopped short, looking around.

"*This* is where they put us?" Rollan asked. "A closet?"

Meilin ran a finger over the sill of the narrow window. It came away coated with dust. "I see they got it ready for us." She pointed at the bed. "Are those sheets clean?"

"Probably not," Abeke said, getting to her feet. The bed creaked alarmingly as she stood up. "What have you two been doing for all this time?"

"Oh, you know, waiting for Essix," Rollan answered. He tapped his chest as a way of telling them the falcon had finally gone into the dormant state. He leaned against the wall as if he was tired, then slid bonelessly to the floor. "Also we spent some time being glared at by those Oathbound guards. And we did some sparring." He nodded at Meilin. "She kicked my butt."

"As usual," Meilin said primly.

"I tried to get her to teach me that throw-the-sword-in-the-air thing she did out there by the gate," Rollan said. "You saw it?"

Abeke and Conor nodded. It had been an amazing move.

"Yeah, well," Rollan went on with a wry grin, "when I tried it I almost cut my own hand off."

Meilin's smug smile turned into a frown as she looked around the room, hands on her hips. "You know, I think this room could be a message for us." Reaching behind her, she closed the door. She crouched on the floor, and the others leaned closer to hear what she would say. "Listen, there's something very strange going on here." Meilin spoke in a near whisper. "It's supposed to be an important meeting of the leaders of the four lands, but it seems as if the Greencloaks are barely tolerated. And they *really* don't like our spirit animals."

Conor nodded. From everything he'd seen in the Citadel, this was true.

"Brunhild—who isn't very merry, by the way—gave us some more trouble on our way here," Abeke put in.

"Not surprising. The Greencloaks have a complicated history," Meilin reminded them. "But even with that, it's weird."

"Maybe we got too comfortable being heroes," Conor said quietly.

Meilin watched him for a moment, her dark eyes pitying. "Maybe," she said, nodding. "But I have to wonder: If they dislike us so much—if they don't believe we are truly heroes—then why did they invite us and the other Greencloaks to the Citadel? What is really going on here?"

4

THE EMPEROR

BEFORE THE OTHERS WERE AWAKE, MEILIN SLIPPED OUT of their tiny room. It was located high in a crumbling tower of the Euran wing of the Citadel. As she descended the spiral staircase, she stretched her arms over her head and worked the kinks out of her back. She had asked the servants for more sleeping pallets, but they'd been little more than thin pads laid over the hard stone floor of the tower room. She didn't want to be stiff and sore if they had challenges to face while they were here.

A few brown-clad servants eyed Meilin as she crossed the entrance hall on the way to the Zhongese part of the Citadel. At those doors, she was stopped by an Oathbound guard, who looked her over suspiciously. Meilin had been well trained as a warrior and as the daughter of a general. She knew how to give orders that would be obeyed. After fixing the Oathbound with a regal glare, he bowed and admitted her. She wanted to talk to Song. The imperial princess had helped the four Greencloaks at the gate. If Meilin was right and something strange *was* going on, then she might be a valuable ally.

As Meilin stepped from the dusty, echoey entrance

hall into the Zhongese section of the Citadel, she paused for a moment, closing her eyes and taking a deep breath. The air was scented with tea and jasmine incense and boiled rice. Smelling it, she felt a sudden, fierce homesickness. It was accompanied by a wave of sorrow for her father, killed on a battlefield during the Second Devourer War.

She and Rollan had been on their way to Jano Rion, the city she'd grown up in, when they'd received the summons from Olvan. They would go back someday soon; maybe Abeke and Conor would come, too.

Opening her eyes, Meilin went on. The Zhongese servants must have been hard at work, for there was no dust in this part of the Citadel, and a glistening carpet covered the stone floor of the passageway. A servant hurried before her, then opened a wooden door carved with Zhongese water dragons, ushering her into a big, bright room hung with embroidered tapestries. The furniture was made of black-lacquered wood and was draped with jewel-toned silk and plump pillows with tassels at every corner. Seated before a low table was Princess Song. A girl stood behind her, putting a last pin into her gleaming black hair.

"Meilin!" the princess exclaimed, jumping to her feet.

Meilin bowed, keeping her face blank. "Your Highness."

Song gestured at the maidservant. "Tea, at once."

To her chagrin, Meilin's stomach growled, loudly. She hadn't had breakfast yet.

"And bring spiced buns," the princess added smoothly, "and some fruit." She seated herself at the low table. "Won't you join me?"

Meilin sat down, feeling uncharacteristically awkward as her sheathed sword bumped the table. The princess was so tiny, so perfect and delicate in her exquisitely embroidered robes. Song wasn't wearing green today, Meilin noted, but purple and deep blue.

"We have met before, haven't we?" Princess Song asked.

Meilin was surprised she remembered it. "Yes, Your Highness. Once. Briefly. A long time ago." Her father had been reporting to the emperor, bringing six-year-old Meilin with him so she could see the vast palaces. A few years older, Princess Song had been like a painted doll. The two girls had played stiffly and politely with the princess's toys, tiny perfect houses with tiny perfect people. Meilin had been reminded of those toys not that long ago when she and her Greencloak friends had gone to the artificially preserved village of Samis in pursuit of the Crystal Polar Bear of Suka.

"I have admired you for a long time," Princess Song said softly.

Meilin swallowed her surprise and called on her lessons in etiquette. One of the main things she had been taught was to conceal her emotions, to be always calm, self-possessed. She raised her eyebrows. "Indeed?" she said carefully.

"Yes." Song fell silent as the servant girl set tea and food on the table and then left the room. "You are a brave and skilled warrior. I know how difficult it is for a Zhongese girl to study the martial arts." She leaned over the table and touched the edge of Meilin's cloak. "And to become a true warrior, as you are. A Greencloak. I have to admit that I envy you."

Meilin felt a sudden burst of sympathy for the other girl. No doubt, as an emperor's daughter, Song led a life of formality and quiet obedience. "We're not just fighters," she said after swallowing a bite of spiced bun, "and it hasn't all been exciting adventures."

"But you have loyal friends at your side," Princess Song said.

Meilin took a drink of hot green tea. The princess, she realized, was lonely. "If you're interested in learning to fight, I could teach you while we're here."

Princess Song's cheeks went pink. "I am afraid . . . it would not be permitted." There was a rush of footsteps outside in the hallway. "But I thank you," she added quickly, and rose gracefully to her feet. "It must be time for the meeting."

Grabbing a spiced bun for each of her friends, Meilin stood, just as the door opened. Two black-clad Oathbound stepped into the room, followed by a big man who could only be the emperor.

He glanced at his daughter and nodded, then looked at Meilin, eyebrows raised. "A Greencloak—here?" he asked in a deep voice.

As Meilin bowed awkwardly, one of the spiced buns bounced out of her hands and rolled across the carpet, coming to a stop at the emperor's feet.

He ignored it. "You are Zhongese?" he asked.

Her face flaming with embarrassment, Meilin answered, "Yes, Your Majesty. I am Meilin, the daughter of General Teng, who died fighting for Zhong during the Second Devourer War."

The emperor nodded. "Your spirit animal is Jhi, the Great Panda."

"Yes, Your Majesty," Meilin answered. She couldn't stop staring at the spiced bun. If he took a step forward, he would squish it.

"The children of Zhong who summon spirit animals should not be given to the Greencloaks," he said grandly.

"Especially when their spirit animals are the very embodiments of our history. They belong to Zhong." And with that pronouncement, he turned and strode out of the room, followed by his loyal Oathbound guards.

"Belong?" Meilin repeated. She wished Rollan was there—he would have a smart answer to the emperor's comment.

"Hurry, Your Highness," called one of the guards. With a quick nod to Meilin, Princess Song rushed out of the room after them.

As she followed them out, Meilin swooped down and grabbed the spiced bun she had dropped.

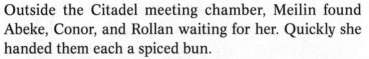

Outside the Citadel meeting chamber, Meilin found Abeke, Conor, and Rollan waiting for her. Quickly she handed them each a spiced bun.

Rollan took a big bite of his, then looked suspiciously at it. "Gritty," he mumbled through his bite.

Meilin gave him a bright smile so he wouldn't suspect that his had been the bun that dropped on the floor.

"What?" he asked.

"Nothing," she said with an innocent blink.

"You're staring at me." Rollan rubbed at his cheek. "I have something on my face, don't I?"

He did, in fact. Meilin still wasn't used to seeing the scar that ran under Rollan's left eye and across his cheek, a wound he'd sustained during the climactic battle to stop the Wyrm. It had faded to pink and now was a thin line of white, but it was a reminder of what he'd been through.

Conor, she noticed, looked tired. His scars weren't like Rollan's—they weren't visible. But they went deeper and would be slower to heal. Meilin hoped he was starting to recover.

Rollan nudged her arm and she looked up to see the leader of the Greencloaks, Olvan, with Lenori at his side; they were followed by a full contingent of Greencloaks, some of whom Meilin recognized and some she didn't.

Other people were starting to gather. Many stared at the Greencloaks as they passed and muttered comments to each other. Meilin saw a proud-looking old man in Niloan garb with a retinue of Oathbound; he had to be the High Chieftain. He was followed into the meeting chamber by the Prime Minister of Amaya and her advisers. The prime minister had a face like a pickled plum, Meilin thought. Wrinkled and sour.

Last came the Queen of Eura, a young woman who was dressed in lace and velvet, with a fur-lined cape. As she crossed the threshold into the meeting chamber, the queen tripped over the edge of her long dress, landing on the floor in a heap of flounces. She shrieked, and three of her courtiers scurried to her side, lifting her to her feet and making soothing noises.

Olvan greeted the young Greencloaks with a nod. He had been taken by the Wyrm, just as Conor had, but he didn't seem to be as weary or troubled as Conor was. Perhaps he only bore the burden more easily. Lenori looked strange without her spirit animal, a gorgeously feathered rainbow ibis, on her shoulder, but she gave them a welcoming smile.

Olvan glanced over at the people streaming into the meeting chamber. "We had better get in there." He placed his hands on Meilin's and Conor's shoulders, drawing them all closer so they could talk without being overheard. "We thought this meeting would be a formality, but it seems there are some serious proposals on the table. Proposals about what to do with the Greencloaks."

Rollan narrowed his eyes. "Have they considered maybe just leaving us alone?"

It was a good question, Meilin thought. "They don't have any authority over us, do they?" she asked.

"These are the leaders of the four major governments of Erdas," Lenori reminded them.

"And Stetriol," Conor put in, pointing out the last leader entering the chamber, a young woman dressed in blue and black—an ambassador from the Council of Stetriol. She wore a pin with a silver *S* on her jacket.

"Right," Olvan said. "Since Zerif used *us* to spread the Wyrm's parasites across Erdas, there have been big changes in the world. These leaders are powerful people, and we have to work with them. Be careful in this meeting." He fixed Rollan with a severe gaze. "And don't say anything."

"I wasn't going to say anything," Rollan muttered.

"Oh, *sure* you weren't," Abeke whispered to him.

The four followed Olvan, Lenori, and the other Greencloaks into the meeting chamber.

The room was massive and echoing. Six stone walls towered over the proceedings, and banners representing each region hung from a very high ceiling; the same flags hung from five of the stone walls. It was more and more significant, Meilin decided, that the Greencloak flag was missing, even though there was a place for it.

In addition to the main entrance, there were doors in each of the walls. Tall windows let in the gray light from outside. In the center of the room was a huge six-sided wooden table. At the table sat the Niloan High Chieftain, the Euran Queen, the Ambassador from Stetriol, and the Amayan Prime Minister, one on each side. At a fifth side sat the Emperor of Zhong, with Princess Song standing quietly beside him. Oathbound guards stood at attention behind all the leaders.

Clearly the sixth side of the table was intended for the Greencloak contingent. There were no chairs.

From the beginning, Meilin had had a bad feeling about this; now the feeling got worse. They were supposed to stand—almost as if they were on trial, and all the lands' leaders were the judges. She saw Olvan and Lenori hesitate for a moment, and then the two Greencloak leaders went to stand at their side of the table, their heads held proudly high. Meilin, Conor, Rollan, and Abeke stood just behind them with the other Greencloaks.

"I will begin," said the oldest of the leaders, the Niloan High Chieftain, "by welcoming you here, to the first meeting between the leaders of the four great lands of Erdas in many, many years. Let us hope that this meeting marks the beginning of a new era of peace and prosperity."

An adviser, standing behind him, leaned over to whisper something into the High Chieftain's ear. He scowled, then nodded. "The four great lands are represented here . . . and Stetriol, of course." His dismissive glance showed what he thought of the island continent that had for so long been an enemy of the other lands. "We have much to discuss," the high chieftain went on. "The first issue on the table . . ." His dark eyes surveyed the room. "What to do about the Greencloak problem."

"Problem?" snorted the Prime Minister of Amaya. "It's more than a simple *problem*."

She definitely resembled a pickled plum, Meilin thought. The woman's mouth was pursed in disapproval, and her nose wrinkled as if she smelled something foul.

"If she's not careful," Rollan leaned over to whisper in Meilin's ear, "her face is going to freeze like that."

Meilin stifled a smile. *"Rollan,"* she chided. They needed to be on their best behavior.

"The Emperor of Zhong has asked to be the first to speak," the high chieftain went on.

The emperor nodded, his mouth set in a severe frown. "The Second Devourer War forced the leaders of Erdas into hiding, where we were protected by our Oathbound guards. Then, just as we emerged to begin rebuilding, another attack began. We heard stories of terrible violence. And this time, who was responsible for this destruction?" He raised his hand and pointed across the table, straight at Olvan. "The Greencloaks."

Beside Meilin, Rollan stirred, as if he was going to protest. She nudged him with her elbow. When he looked over at her, she shook her head. He gave a slight nod.

She knew he didn't like it. Neither did she. But she had a feeling that speaking now would just make things worse.

The emperor went on, his deep voice filling the room. "The very leader of the Greencloaks was taken by the Wyrm, spreading its corruption. As a group beholden to no nation, but with unparalleled access to all of them, they spread this corruption farther than any other force could have. It is clear to everyone here: The Greencloaks have become too powerful, and far too dangerous."

"This is true," the Amayan Prime Minister added in a sharp voice. "They cannot be trusted."

The Ambassador from Stetriol had a soft voice, but somehow she made herself heard. "We in Stetriol," she began, as the others fell silent to listen, "have good reason to hate the Greencloaks, who for so long denied us the Nectar that would have prevented the bonding sickness. And yet . . ." Serenely, she looked around the room, making sure everyone was listening. "And yet we see the Greencloaks now as allies. With their aid, Stetriol is at last taking its proper place in the world—no longer outcast, no longer forgotten. We value the Greencloaks. For us, they are not a *problem*, but a solution."

Meilin felt like cheering at the ambassador's words.

But the other leaders, even the wide-eyed Euran queen, were starting to look like the prime minister: They were making that disapproving pickled-plum face.

The high chieftain was nodding. "Speaking of the the oh-so-precious Nectar. We all know that the Greencloaks jealously guarded the secret of its creation. Only *they* were allowed to administer its protective power. But now the Nectar Ceremony doesn't exist," the high chieftain said. "The Nectar of Ninani is no longer needed. The Greencloaks, too, are not needed as they once were."

"Exactly," boomed the emperor, and slammed a fist onto the table, claiming everyone's attention. "And so I propose that the Greencloaks should be disbanded."

Meilin gasped aloud. There were murmurs and nods of agreement from the other leaders. Except for the Ambassador from Stetriol, who frowned and gazed down at the tabletop.

The emperor went inexorably on. "Each of the Marked must be returned to their own nations, to serve their proper lords."

So that's what the emperor had meant by *belong*, Meilin realized. She found herself shaking her head. Looking aside, she saw the same denial on Abeke's face. Beside her, Conor had gone pale. Break up the Greencloaks? This was *wrong*. So, so wrong.

But they had been ordered to stay silent. Olvan was the Greencloaks' leader; he would speak for them.

To Meilin's dismay, Olvan's head had lost its proud tilt, and he was staring at the floor as if he couldn't think of a response. Beside him, Lenori looked troubled. It was true that some of the Greencloaks, including Olvan, had fallen prey to the Wyrm, but they had served it against their will. *And* they had defeated it, in the end. *That* is what Olvan should tell the leaders.

But it was Princess Song who spoke next. Standing just behind the emperor's chair, she looked so small, like a child, and almost fragile. But when she spoke, her voice did not have the soft, sweet tones of a well-bred Zhongese girl. Instead, she sounded like a true leader.

"I disagree with my father," she said firmly. All the other leaders stopped their stirring to stare at her. The emperor's face went as still as stone. He folded his arms across his chest, as if denying his daughter's words.

The princess went bravely on. "Have you forgotten that the Greencloaks saved the entire world?"

"Twice," Meilin heard Rollan whisper.

"If not for the Greencloaks, the Devourer and his Conquerors would have destroyed everyone in this room," Song declared. "We owe them our lives. We owe them a place of honor in this remade world!"

Her words rang out, and the room fell into utter silence.

Then her father pushed back his chair and got to his feet, his face a mask of anger. Deliberately he stepped in front of Princess Song, blocking her from the table. "My daughter speaks without permission," he snapped. "The words of a disobedient girl mean nothing. Do not listen to them."

"We cannot break up the Greencloaks!" Princess Song insisted.

Her father whirled to face her, fury in every line of his body.

Meilin found she was holding her breath.

But before the emperor could act, all six doors leading into the meeting chamber banged open at the same time, the sounds echoing from the stone walls.

In each doorway stood a man or a woman wearing a green cloak.

They were here to help, Meilin thought, feeling relieved. They would speak to the leaders of Erdas about the Greencloaks' heroic actions in the wars.

One by one, the green-cloaked figures brought their spirit animals out of their passive states. A hyena crouched at the feet of one, wild-eyed and drooling. A bat swooped over the head of another. There was a raptor of some kind; a small, lithe pantherlike cat; and a white rat with glittering pink eyes.

As one, the Greencloaks in the doorways drew their swords.

Wait. Were they going to . . . ?

Before Meilin could shout out a warning, the Greencloaks and their animal companions hurled themselves into an attack.

There were screams. The room erupted into chaos.

BETRAYAL

"WHAT ARE THEY *DOING*?" ABEKE BLURTED OUT AS THE attackers stormed into the room.

Rollan glanced at her. Abeke's eyes were wide and horrified.

"It looks like—" He broke off. "They're Greencloaks, aren't they?"

Rollan looked around wildly, seeing one of the green-cloaked figures stalk into the room. Her lithe, pantherlike jaguarundi, an animal from Amaya, crouched and then leaped toward the Ambassador of Stetriol, snarling. There was a shrill scream. Some of the leaders were shouting for the Oathbound guards to protect them. Another one of the attackers slashed with his sword, and blood spurted from the chest of one of the queen's courtiers.

"Who *are* they?" Conor gasped, drawing his ax.

"We can't fight them," Rollan said, shaking his head. "They're Greencloaks."

At the table, Olvan had called forth his spirit animal. The mighty moose tossed its antlers, sending the white rat flying. "Call forth your spirit animals!" Olvan roared at the other Greencloaks. "Defend the leaders!"

Meilin was the first to leap into action. Ripping her sword from its sheath, she dove, sliding across the surface of the six-sided table just in time to stop the jaguarundi from advancing on Princess Song.

Roughly, Meilin grabbed Song and shoved her under the table.

"Stay there!" she shouted—and took up a defensive stance. If the invaders wanted to get to the princess, they would have to go through her. A moment later, Jhi was at her side.

Conor had already brought Briggan out of his dormant state. The wolf leaped and intercepted the hyena in midair. There was a crash of bone and fur and the gnashing of teeth.

Beside Rollan, Abeke had strung her bow and was taking careful aim at one of the invaders' spirit animals, a huge bat with leathery wings that was swooping down and scratching at the eyes of anyone defending the leaders.

"Let Essix get it!" Rollan shouted to her, calling forth the falcon. As Essix streaked across the room toward the bat, Abeke nodded, then she searched out another target. Rollan heard Uraza's roar as the great leopard came out of passive state.

All around Rollan was chaos, snarling, and screams. People stumbled past with blood streaming from their wounds. He caught a quick glimpse of Meilin, relieved to see her on her feet, still protecting the princess. Wielding his long knife, he cleared a space around Abeke so she could take aim without worrying about being attacked.

He blocked a thrust from one of the green-cloaked invaders, then kicked at the white rat, which was coming at him with its teeth bared.

There was a lull in the fighting. Everything fell suddenly into quiet while attackers and defenders caught their breaths and decided their next moves. In the silence, the Emperor of Zhong stepped onto a chair and then onto the top of the six-sided table.

"Betrayers!" he thundered, pointing at the invaders. "The Greencloaks have shown what they truly are. *Betrayers!*"

As if in answer, there was a growl from across the room. The steep-shouldered hyena, bleeding from where Briggan had slashed it with his sharp teeth, sprang past Meilin, past Olvan. It snarled, leaped onto the table, and tore out the emperor's throat.

All watched in stunned horror as the emperor staggered back, blood spraying from his neck, and collapsed onto the tabletop. Rollan couldn't even move. It had happened so suddenly.

The hyena bayed with bloody fangs, a howl of triumph.

It was answered by a shrill whistle—a signal—and the green-cloaked invaders and their spirit animals headed for the main exit, slashing and stabbing at anyone who got in their way. They plunged through the doorway. One of Abeke's arrows thudded into the door just as it slammed behind them.

The room was thick with blood and the moans of the wounded. Several people were shouting.

The ones doing most of the shouting, Rollan realized, were the Oathbound. He hadn't noticed them in the fight, but they must have defended the leaders.

He saw Meilin on the other side of the table, bending to help Princess Song out of her hiding place. Meilin tried to turn Song away from the sight of her father's body, but the princess had a will of iron. She said something to Meilin and then jerked herself away.

Taking a deep breath, the princess pointed at a tipped-over chair. The Oathbound guard leader, Brunhild the Merry, leaped to set it upright.

Brunhild gave Song her hand, helping her to step onto the surface of the table.

"I must speak again," Princess Song began, her voice steady. All in the room stopped what they were doing and turned to listen. She stood there, her hair tousled, her gown torn, a smear of blood across one pale cheek. At her feet, her father's body lay in a pool of blood that was already growing sticky. Yet she did not waver. "In this attack, the Greencloaks have shown their true colors. Not green." She bent to touch the table, then stood and held up her hand, which was covered with her father's blood. "Their true color is red. Bloodred. My father was right. We have seen what they are—traitors."

The princess stared at her own blood-smeared hand, and finally her control broke. She fell to her knees beside her father's body and wept. With a tearstained face, she pointed straight at Olvan and Lenori. "Oathbound, don't let the rest of the Greencloaks escape," she ordered. "Arrest them at once!"

VENOM

CONOR KNEW ROLLAN WELL ENOUGH TO KNOW WHAT he was going to do. "No time to argue," he told his friend. Briggan bounded to his side, panting, his fur spotted with blood.

"But–" Rollan protested, gripping his knife.

"We can't fight them," Conor said. He sheathed his ax.

On the other side of the table, the Oathbound were gathering. Brunhild pointed at the remaining Greencloaks. As a group, they started across the room, drawing their swords, while Brunhild, four steps behind them, called forth her spirit animal, the stone viper.

"No, don't," Conor said, grabbing Abeke's hand to stop her from drawing the last arrow from her quiver. "It'll just prove what the princess said. We have to get out of here!"

The black-clad Oathbound guards were closing in, seizing the remaining Greencloaks and forcing them to the floor. Lenori's spirit animal, the brightly colored ibis, perched on her shoulder and spread its wings, a distraction to the guards. Lenori, who hated violence of any kind, stepped forward with her hands raised, trying to explain to the guards that they had not been part of the attack.

"Arrest the Greencloaks!" shouted Brunhild.

As Princess Song issued crisp commands, Olvan put his moose into passive state and gathered up Conor, Abeke, and Rollan; Meilin was still on the other side of the table. "You cannot be captured." He started clearing their way to the door. "Come!"

"Meilin!" Rollan shouted, pointing at the door. Conor saw Meilin nod and then sheathe her sword. Jhi, huge and implacable, lumbered into two approaching Oathbound soldiers, giving Meilin a path of escape.

When they got to the door, Meilin quickly called Jhi into passive state. Olvan shoved them all outside, leaving Lenori and the other Greencloaks to hold off their pursuers. He almost caught Essix's tail feathers in the door when he slammed it closed.

"To my room—the Euran wing," he ordered. "Hurry!" Bringing his spirit animal out of the passive state again, he left the moose to guard the door while he and the others sprinted down the hallway that led to the Euran wing of the Citadel. As they fled, Conor heard the sound of the moose trumpeting a challenge, and then the clatter of running feet coming after them.

Breathless, they reached Olvan's set of rooms, all decorated in a style very familiar to Conor—they looked like Devin Trunswick's rooms back home in Eura.

When they were all inside, Olvan quickly closed the door, locked it, and turned to face the kids.

Briggan crouched at Conor's side, his tongue lolling. Essix was nowhere to be seen, but Rollan didn't look worried, so Conor knew the independent falcon was safe. Uraza was sleek gold and black as she padded around the edge of the room, sniffing at the heavy wooden furniture.

Conor noticed that Meilin was very pale. He saw Rollan edge closer, so his arm was touching hers. She swallowed and then clenched her teeth, as if holding in tears. Then he remembered that she'd seen her own father cut down on the battlefield—maybe the death of the emperor was making her relive that awful moment.

"All those Greencloaks were new recruits," Olvan said, striding across the room to a carved chest. The box sat under a window with lots of tiny, diamond-shaped panes.

"Not *Green*cloaks," Rollan said angrily. "*Fake*cloaks."

Shaking off her distraction, Meilin nodded. "They were impersonating Greencloaks to make us seem like criminals."

Abeke was busy checking the string on her bow. "But who are they, really?" she asked, looking up. "Who sent them? Who hates the Greencloaks that much?"

"The emperor," Rollan answered. "Who's dead."

"Less chatter," Olvan ordered, opening the chest under the window. "The Oathbound are just behind us. Meilin is right—there is no coincidence that this happened in front of the leaders of Erdas. Someone is trying to sabotage the Greencloaks. Lenori and I are certain to be blamed for this attack, and arrested."

As if confirming his words, there was a rush of footsteps out in the hallway. A moment later came a loud banging on the door. "Open up!" shouted a booming voice.

"You four have a chance to get away," Olvan said hurriedly, tossing clothes out of the chest, searching for something. "There is something you must do." He paused.

"Ah, here it is." From the chest he took a cloth-wrapped object, about the size of a baby's fist. "For many years, this gift has been passed down from one leader of the Greencloaks to the next. There is a saying associated with it: *When Greencloak fights Greencloak, that which is hidden must be revealed.*"

The door to the room shuddered under the blows of the guards trying to get in. The wood around the lock was starting to splinter.

"And now that warning has come to pass. Greencloak has fought Greencloak." Olvan held out the small bundle to Meilin. "Take it."

"What are we supposed to do with it?" Meilin said, taking the gift and shoving it into a little pouch that she wore on her belt.

Olvan was about to answer when Conor noticed that silence had fallen out in the hallway. He turned and saw a slim flicker of brown slither through the crack at the base of the door.

The stone viper—the spirit animal of Brunhild the Merry!

"Look out!" he shouted. He seized Abeke's arm and pulled her away.

"What?" Rollan asked, looking for a threat coming through the door.

"Snake!" Conor pointed at the floor. "It's fast! Don't let it bite you!"

Briggan growled, on guard. "No!" Conor yelled. He gripped Abeke's arm. "Don't let Uraza near it," he said urgently, and she immediately grabbed the scruff of the leopard's neck, holding her back.

The snake was no bigger than a pencil, but moved with terrifying speed. As the Greencloaks backed away, the stone viper darted to the middle of the room and paused, its tongue flickering, sensing the location of each body in the room.

"Quick!" Olvan called, gesturing to another door. "Go that way. Straight along the passage, second right, then down the first set of stairs you come to. It'll take you to the Citadel walls."

As she hustled toward the door, Meilin asked her question again: "Olvan, what are we supposed to do with the gift?"

"Reveal it," Olvan responded. He was about to add something when the snake made its choice.

Moving with lightning speed, it struck like an arrow, sinking its fangs into Olvan's leg, just above his boot.

Conor gasped as the viper's poison already began to take hold. First Olvan's leg froze in a rigid stance, then his other leg, and then his arms.

Olvan spoke quickly as the stone venom crept over his chest. "You must find out who is trying to break apart the Greencloaks," he wheezed. As he spoke, the poison crept up his neck to attack his face, turning his skin gray and pale. His breath rasped. "The same . . . force will try to divide you." His voice slurred, his mouth hardly able to move. "Stay true to . . . each . . ."

The four kids stared in horror as the poison overcame Olvan. The big man's body wobbled off balance, then he tipped over and crashed onto the floor. His green cloak settled over him.

At the same moment, the door splintered under the blows of the Oathbound guards.

7

ANKA

"COME ON!" MEILIN SHOUTED, FLINGING OPEN THE DOOR Olvan had said led to a way out of the Citadel. "It's clear," she said over her shoulder. "Let's go!"

"What about Olvan?" Conor protested as the Oathbound fought their way past the door they'd broken open.

Rollan's heart lurched at the thought of leaving Olvan behind. But they had to flee. "We can't help him now," he answered, grabbing Conor and checking to see that Abeke was coming. "He told us to escape, so that's what we have to do."

Snarling, Briggan and Uraza held off the Oathbound guards as the kids made it out of the room, then raced down the hallway.

"Olvan said we should turn at the second right," Abeke called, a step behind Rollan.

"Second *left*," Meilin corrected, and they pelted around a corner. Bounding, Briggan caught up to them, followed by Uraza, silent and deadly.

"Are you sure it's left?" Conor panted.

"No!" Meilin shot back.

They reached a crossroads where two passageways met. Meilin looked right, then frantically left. From behind them came the sounds of pursuit, growing louder.

"I'm pretty sure it was straight," Conor put in.

And then, suddenly, someone else had joined them.

"Gah!" Meilin shouted.

Rollan was used to seeing better than anyone, thanks to his connection to Essix, but the Greencloak who appeared at Meilin's shoulder had come out of nowhere. It was a woman, he could see that much. But her features were oddly blurred and . . . was her skin gray? Like the stone walls of the passageway?

"Where did *you* come from?" Rollan demanded.

"I've been here the whole time," the mysterious Greencloak answered, "and I'm here to help. This way." She pointed at a door that they hadn't noticed, then flung it open and started down a set of stairs.

No, Rollan was certain. The door had *not* been there before! Had this Greencloak hidden it somehow?

Briggan growled. The Oathbound were after them. Rollan could hear their footsteps coming from Olvan's room.

"Hurry!" called the Greencloak woman. "I can hide you!"

"Who *are* you?" panted Meilin as the four kids, Briggan, and Uraza rushed out of the passageway and onto the stairs, Conor quietly closing the door behind them.

"Shhhh," hissed the Greencloak. "Shut up for half a moment, if you can."

Rollan *so* wanted to snipe at her for that comment, but he saw the wisdom of staying quiet. The stairs were dark; even Rollan's keen eyes couldn't make out more than shadows. Their panting breaths sounded loud in the silence.

"Won't they just open the door and come after us?" Meilin whispered to Rollan.

He shrugged, even though he knew she couldn't see him in the dark. He was starting to suspect what the mysterious Greencloak's spirit animal might be. If he was right, the guards wouldn't even see the door.

From above came the sound of the Oathbound pursuers. Their feet pounding, they ran straight past the closed door.

Yep. Rollan's guess was right.

"Come on," whispered the Greencloak woman from ahead. "Follow me, and stay absolutely quiet."

They did as she'd ordered, Conor putting Briggan into passive state and Uraza padding on stealthy paws at their backs. Essix, Rollan knew, was waiting for them outside, circling high above the Citadel.

At the bottom of the stairs they turned right, down another long, dark passage. At its end was a doorway leading to a courtyard, and then the outer wall of the Citadel. Rollan could hear shouts in the distance: the Oathbound guards searching for Greencloaks to arrest. A booming echo was the portcullis at the front gate slamming closed. They definitely weren't getting out that way. As he watched, two brown-clad servants rushed across the courtyard. The entire Citadel was stirred up, on the alert. Escaping was going to be impossible.

Unless . . .

In the light of the doorway, Rollan got his first really good look at the new Greencloak. She seemed to have dark hair in a long braid down her back, and skin the same light brown as his own.

"Weren't you . . . grayer before?" Rollan whispered to her.

She shot him an annoyed glare. "Yeah, they warned me about you," she said sharply.

"The smart one?" Rollan asked.

"Smart *mouth*, more like," she whispered back.

Rollan found himself grinning. He liked her already. "Chameleon spirit animal, right?"

He saw a flash of surprise cross her face. Then she gave a brusque nod. Rollan caught a glimpse of a small lizard-ish shape on her shoulder, blending in with the green of her cloak. Chameleon. Without the keen sight he got from his bond with Essix, he never would have noticed it. "What's your name?" he asked.

"Anka," she answered.

Meilin joined them. "I assume we're getting out that way," she whispered, pointing at a door in the outer wall of the Citadel, across a stone-paved courtyard. "But how are we going to get over there without being spotted?" As she spoke, two Oathbound guards clattered into the courtyard, swords drawn, clearly searching for the escaping Greencloaks. After seeing that the area was deserted, the guards rushed away.

"Now," Anka whispered. "Quickly. If I say *still*, stand against the wall and don't move." She turned her glare on Rollan. "And don't talk. Don't even breathe."

"But—" Meilin began to protest. Rollan knew her—she wanted explanations.

But they didn't have time. "Just do it," Anka said, and Rollan nodded to reassure Meilin.

Abeke had put Uraza into passive state, and the four kids, led by the mysterious Greencloak, Anka, started around the edge of the courtyard, keeping close to the stone walls that enclosed it. Behind them, the Citadel buzzed with activity.

They were halfway around the courtyard, ten steps away from the gate in the outer wall, when they heard the sound of Oathbound guards approaching—from the passageway they'd just left!

"*Still!*" came Anka's swift order.

Obeying, Rollan flattened himself against the wall, his shoulder against Meilin's, Anka beside him. He knew Conor and Abeke had done it, too. Not one of them moved.

Don't even breathe, he told himself.

The two Oathbound took several steps into the courtyard, looking around. Their eyes passed right over Rollan and the others, but they didn't react.

Without moving his head, Rollan looked aside at Meilin. He knew she was there, and his Essix-enhanced eyes had keener vision than most, but all he could see of her was the faintest of outlines. Thanks to Anka's chameleon spirit animal, all five of them were invisible— they had blended right into the wall.

"They're not here," one of the Oathbound guards said, turning away. "Let's check the other passageway."

"Wait," said the other, a tall man with a broad, handsome, brown-skinned face, framed by flowing black hair.

Rollan realized that the man was Marked. He carried his spirit animal in the crook of his arm—it was a fluffy, brown, almost wingless bird that had two nostril holes at the end of a long, thin beak. It was a kiwi bird, from a small island near Stetriol, and it had a dangerously keen sense of smell.

Which meant the Oathbound who held it might not be able to *see* them, but his nose might tell him they were there.

Trying not to move, Rollan sniffed the air to see if he could smell himself. Uh-oh. He should have taken a bath at the last inn. The others were probably just as stinky.

In the center of the courtyard, the Marked Oathbound had closed his eyes and stood drawing in the air through his nose. The kiwi in his arms blinked its tiny black eyes.

Rollan held his breath.

Frowning, the Marked Oathbound opened his eyes again and looked carefully around the courtyard. He sniffed and took a step closer to where they were hidden.

"They're not here," his partner said impatiently.

"They *were* here," the Marked Oathbound said. "And not that long ago, either." Another sniff, and he shrugged. "But I don't see them. We'd better report in."

Rollan let out a relieved breath as the two guards hurried away.

At his side, Abeke looked confused. "He looked right at us," she whispered.

Rollan opened his mouth to explain.

"Let's go," Anka interrupted, and started off before checking to be sure the kids were following.

Quietly, the five of them slipped through the door in the wall and into the forest that surrounded the Citadel. For a while they could hear the uproar as the rest of the Greencloaks were arrested and the Citadel was being searched, but the noise soon fell away behind them. They padded on quiet feet through a shadowy forest, where the ground was thickly carpeted with pine needles. Ferns brushed at their knees, and the high branches of the pine trees cut off the light.

"All right, that's far enough," Meilin said, stopping.

Rollan went to stand at her side, along with Abeke and Conor, who had brought their spirit animals out of passive state. Briggan sat at Conor's side, and Uraza crouched at Abeke's feet, looking ready to pounce. Essix, he knew, was perched in a tree nearby, watching.

Anka turned to face them. Her skin, Rollan noticed, had taken on a greenish tinge, making her blend into the forest. "Weren't you . . . browner before?" he asked her.

She shot him an annoyed look.

He grinned back at her. Having Anka around to aggravate was going to be fun.

"You're a Greencloak?" Meilin asked Anka, beginning the questions.

Anka turned to show off the green cloak she wore. "Obviously."

"There's nothing obvious about it," Meilin shot back. "At the meeting in the Citadel, there was an attack by Greencloaks. Olvan said they were new recruits. And we've never seen you before. How do we know we can trust you? How do we know you're not one of those false Greencloaks?"

"Fakecloaks," Rollan put in.

"I've been around," Anka said, folding her arms. "You just never noticed me."

Abeke made the connection. "Oh, I get it. The way the guards didn't notice us in the courtyard. Chameleon spirit animal?"

Anka gave a smug nod.

"Can we see him?" Abeke asked. She turned and spoke to Conor. "Chameleons are really cute. Have you ever seen one before?"

Conor shook his head. "Never."

"Toey is shy," Anka said, her usually sharp voice softening for the first time. "You might catch a glimpse of him now and then."

Meilin still looked suspicious. Rollan caught her eye. "She's telling the truth, as far as I can see," he told her. "I think we can trust her."

"Oh, *thank* you," Anka said sarcastically. "I save you from the Citadel and you *think* you can trust me?"

"We've seen betrayal before." Meilin's face was serious. She patted the pouch where she'd put the gift from Olvan. "And we have a mission. We can't be too careful."

Rollan saw Briggan prick up his ears and then nudge Conor's leg with his nose. In response, Conor cocked his head, listening. "Uh, we'd better keep moving. I think the Citadel has sent somebody after us."

"Oathbound," Anka told them. "They're expert trackers—we have to go. *Now.*"

SECRETS REVEALED

THE OATHBOUND WERE RELENTLESS.

They tracked the five Greencloaks all afternoon, never giving them time to rest or even catch their breaths. Abeke was glad she'd spent the months after the defeat of the Wyrm hunting in Nilo. It meant she could run for a long time without getting tired.

As the sun set and the forest grew darker and colder, Abeke followed Anka through the pine trees, Uraza at her side and Meilin a step behind. Next came Rollan, with Conor and Briggan bringing up the rear.

The sounds of pursuit had fallen away behind them, but Abeke knew the Oathbound were following. Still, they had to rest sometime. Anka couldn't keep leading them on through the entire night. Or could she?

Abeke paused and let Rollan and Meilin pass her, and then fell into step beside Conor. Uraza and Briggan trailed behind them. "I keep thinking about Olvan," Abeke whispered. The last they'd seen of the Greencloak leader, he'd fallen to the floor after being bitten by the Oathbound leader's stone viper. "The snake's poison," she went on. "Do you think it killed him?"

"There is an antidote," Conor responded. He shot her a worried look. "They would give it to him, wouldn't they? They wouldn't let him die?"

"I hope not," Abeke said grimly. She wished she could go back to the Citadel and help Olvan, but she knew that all they could do was try to fulfill the mission he'd given them. If they could figure out what they were supposed to do.

She checked Conor and saw he looked pale. Dark smudges under his eyes showed how tired he was. Because of the nightmares, he hadn't had enough sleep for weeks. Or for even longer—not since he had been taken by the Wyrm. He couldn't keep up this pace. But she knew he wouldn't complain.

They walked on as night fell and a full moon rose above the forest, bright enough that they could see where they were going. Silver-edged shadows lurked beyond the path, and a cold breeze blew through the branches overhead.

After another hour of walking without the sounds of Oathbound pursuers, Anka called a halt. The four kids gathered around her. "Meilin," Anka said, keeping her voice low, "you said you have a mission. We need to know where we're going."

Meilin gave a weary sigh. "I have no idea what Olvan wanted us to do." She took the cloth-wrapped gift out of the pouch. "He gave us this and said it had to be *revealed*, whatever that means." Carefully, she unwrapped the gift.

In the pale moonlight, it looked like . . .

"It's a *rock*," Rollan said.

Abeke tossed her braids over her shoulder and leaned closer to see. He was right. It was a scaly-looking black rock about the size of a baby's fist.

"Ah." Anka reached out a finger to touch the rock, then drew back. "I know what this is, and what you're supposed to do with it."

"*How* do you know?" Meilin asked suspiciously.

"You may not have noticed me before," Anka said, "but I am a Greencloak. And I know some secrets that have not been revealed to you."

"But you're going to reveal them now, right?" Rollan put in.

Anka looked around at the dark forest. There was no sound of pursuit. "We can sit and rest for a few minutes, and I'll tell you."

Relieved, Abeke and the other kids sank wearily to the ground. Uraza crouched close beside Abeke. Essix had flown down to perch on a nearby branch. The moonlight filtered between the trees, pushing back the shadows. Despite the light, Abeke could barely make out Anka's figure; thanks to her chameleon spirit animal, she blended in with the night.

Anka spoke from the shadows. "This rock is not what it appears to be. It's one of a set of four items precious to the Greencloaks. Olvan knew this. Why didn't he tell you when he gave it to you?"

"We didn't exactly have time," Conor said. At his side, Briggan flopped down to lie with his big head on Conor's foot.

Anka nodded, understanding. "Olvan would have told you that long ago, the four regions of Erdas bestowed the Greencloaks with gifts as thanks for ending the First Devourer War. Four items wielded by four ancient heroes of Erdas–"

"Four items," Rollan put in, "wielded by four heroes?"

"Don't interrupt," Anka said sharply.

"Yeah, but I can't help but notice that me, Conor, Abeke, and Meilin add up to four," Rollan said.

"And you didn't even have to count on your fingers," Anka sniped. "Now be quiet so I can tell you the rest." She paused, then shrugged. "But it probably is important that there are four of you, each from a different region. It makes sense that this quest would fall to you. Anyway, the four gifts were symbols that the Greencloaks were of and for *all* Erdas."

"Not broken up, as the leaders seem to want now," Meilin observed.

"No," Anka said. "Greencloaks united. Loyal to each other. Willing to serve all nations."

"So, back to the rock that is more than it seems," Rollan reminded her.

"Yes." Anka pointed to the rock. "As its gift, Amaya sent a legendary polished jewel called the Heart of the Land. As you can see, it's been disguised somehow, and it must be revealed. Zhong gave something called the Dragon's Eye. Nilo and Eura gave gifts, too, but I can't remember their names. The gifts, all except for the Heart, have been hidden."

"And we have to find them," Abeke realized. "If there are four gifts that are meant to show the four lands that the Greencloaks are for everyone, then we need to find them all."

"We should reveal the Heart first," Meilin said. "Like Olvan ordered. The only question is how?"

"Amaya," Anka said softly. "I don't know much, but there's a place in the region that's connected to the gift."

"Wait a minute," Rollan said, pointing at the rock. "We have this object, right? And we're supposed to collect these other objects and use them to save the world? Sounds familiar, doesn't it?"

"No," Meilin answered. "Before, the Greencloaks had to save the world—"

"Twice," Abeke and Conor said at the same time.

"But this time," Meilin went on, "*for* the world, we have to save the Greencloaks." She held out the rock, a dark lump in her hand. "So we'll take up this quest to reveal the Heart of the Land and then find all the gifts?" she asked.

"Yes," Abeke said without hesitating, putting her hand onto Meilin's, feeling the rough surface of the rock under her palm.

"Yes," Conor agreed, putting his hand over hers.

"Definitely," Rollan said, and put his hand on the top.

"For the Greencloaks," Meilin said solemnly.

"For the Greencloaks," Abeke, Conor, and Rollan repeated.

Abeke looked around at her friends, the three people she trusted most in the world. Anka, she realized, had faded completely away. For a moment, Abeke felt sorry for her. The chameleon made it so she was always around, but never noticed.

Then Abeke's keen senses went on the alert. While they'd been talking, the wind had stilled and the forest had grown completely silent. Too silent. Fog was creeping in, flowing like long, white snakes between the tree trunks.

Anka appeared again, standing a few paces farther down the path. She whirled to face the kids. "We've stopped for too long. The Oathbound are coming."

Abeke leaped up. "We can't let them catch us."

As she stood, Meilin wrapped up the Heart of the Land. She quickly stowed it in her belt pouch.

Abeke checked Conor. He was getting to his feet slowly. "Are you all right?" she asked him.

"I'm fine," he answered, but she didn't think he was.

Essix took off from her branch, quickly disappearing into the night. "So we're heading for Amaya?" Rollan asked.

"Less talking, more running away," Anka said, appearing at his side. "They're coming. Let's go!"

Wearily slinging her bow over her shoulder, Abeke got ready to run for the rest of the night.

WIKAM THE JUST

THE ROCK WASN'T HEAVY, BUT MEILIN FELT THE BURDEN of carrying it.

For three days and three nights they traveled through the forest, with the Oathbound in pursuit. Anka led them along the southern coast of Eura, heading for a port where they could get a ship to Amaya. The Oathbound wouldn't be able to track them over the sea, so they'd be free to reveal the rock and find the other three gifts that had come down to them from the time of legends.

But the four Greencloaks and Anka still had to get away from their pursuers. They slept only in snatches, with one person on guard, until all of them felt so weary it was like they were carrying loads of bricks on their backs.

One day at sunset, they stopped in a clearing in a pine forest to eat a cold dinner—they made no fire to give them away to the trackers—and huddled together, shivering, as the twilight advanced. During the day Anka had left them for a time, to slip into a village and buy supplies. At least, Meilin hoped she'd paid for the food;

with her chameleon spirit animal, Anka would probably make a very good thief. Maybe that was why Rollan seemed to like her so much, despite her sharp voice and her short temper.

"What am I eating?" Rollan asked, inspecting the food Anka had given him.

"Meat," she answered.

"I don't even want to ask this question," Rollan said, taking a bite, "but what kind of meat?"

"The chewy kind," Anka answered.

"Mmm," Rollan mumbled. "My favorite."

Conor, Meilin noticed, had fallen asleep already, with his head on Abeke's shoulder, his dinner uneaten.

Meilin was glad for Jhi's warm, furry bulk at her back. With a sigh, she ate her serving of "meat" and a hard biscuit, and listened to Rollan and Anka talking.

"So this quest we're on. How do we reveal what is hidden?" Rollan asked. He shifted closer, so his shoulder was touching Meilin's.

"Greencloak lore says that the rock is called the *Heart of the Land*," Anka answered. "And it comes from Amaya, where there is a place called the Heart of the Land. An island in the middle of the large lake that lies to the northeast of Concorba."

"Yeah, I've heard of the lake," Rollan said. "So we have to go there?"

"It's the most likely place." Anka's voice answered, but Meilin couldn't see the young woman anymore; she'd faded away as the forest grew darker.

"Can we rest here tonight?" Abeke whispered. "Conor needs to sleep some more."

Anka didn't answer, so Meilin spoke for her. "We'll stay for as long as we can."

They sat quietly for a few minutes. As the sun set completely, the moon rose, flooding the clearing with silvery light.

"If the rock is from Amaya," Rollan asked, "and *I* am from Amaya, why didn't Olvan give it to me to carry?"

"Because I'm the responsible one," Meilin said, smiling to herself.

Rollan bumped her shoulder with his, and she heard him laugh.

Then it occurred to her that maybe Rollan *should* be the one carrying the Heart of the Land. She sat up. "Anka said the four gifts were *wielded* by four heroes. That means they must have some power, don't you think?"

Anka answered from the shadows. "It is likely that the gifts are more than just symbols. We just don't know what power they have."

Meilin dug the rock from her pouch and unwrapped it. "Here," she said, holding it out to Rollan. "Take it." When he did, she asked, "Do you feel anything? Any connection? Any power?"

Rollan closed his hand around the bumpy rock, waiting to see if anything happened. "Nope," he answered at last. "Nothing."

"Because it's hidden. It hasn't been revealed yet," Anka said impatiently. "Until then it really is just a rock."

Rollan handed it back to Meilin, and she put it away again. She leaned back against Jhi, who sighed and shifted to make herself more comfortable. Looking up at the sky, she saw the pinpricks of stars. Something drifted across her vision. It was a faint thread, glinting in the moonlight. Sleepily, she watched it unspool across the clearing. Then another silvery thread floated past, just overhead. They looked like silk. So pretty.

Across from her, Conor jerked awake. "They're coming," he blurted.

Meilin sat up and listened. She heard nothing but the wind in the trees. "Are you sure?" Maybe it was another one of Conor's bad dreams.

Abeke was getting to her feet, checking her bow and quiver, which had just one arrow in it. "Yes, he's sure," she said, as Conor stood up with Briggan beside him.

Meilin stood as well, then offered her hand to Rollan. She hauled him to his feet. "I don't hear anything," he said.

"Shhh," cautioned Anka. "They could be sneaking up on us. Put your animals into passive state. We'll go quietly, and I'll hide us, just in case."

Without speaking, the five Greencloaks left the clearing. Meilin led the way. Thanks to Anka's chameleon, when Meilin glanced over her shoulder to check on the others, they all looked like nothing more than shadows gliding through the darkness. Essix, who refused to go into passive state unless it was absolutely necessary, flew from branch to branch. The falcon flew on silent wings and wouldn't give them away.

The path was like a dark tunnel before them. Meilin paced along it, trying to stay quiet. As she walked, a thin thread of spidersilk broke across her face. She brushed it away and kept going.

Then, ahead, she saw an entire spiderweb stretched across the path. It was about the size of a shield, and it glinted in the moonlight. A little dark blob of a spider sat in its center.

Meilin was *not* afraid of spiders. At least, that's what she told herself. Ever since she and Abeke had seen Shane's sister, Drina, killed by her own spider spirit animal, she'd felt a little queasy about them. And then there had been the Webmother in the dark passages of Sadre. She tried to think of spiders as mice. Cute, furry, baby mice that happened to have eight legs and completely creepy eyes. And fangs . . .

As Meilin cautiously approached the web, she reached to sweep it out of her way. But the threads were like glue—they stuck to her arm. Two more steps, and another web appeared in her path, at the same height as her head. Before she could duck, she'd stepped into it—and the sticky threads wrapped around her face like a net. *"Ick,"* she whispered.

She stumbled to a halt, trying to wipe the web out of her eyes.

"What's the matter?" Rollan whispered, right behind her.

"I'm just . . . stuck!" she answered. Finally she managed to scrape it away, just in time to see something plummet from the trees and land at Rollan's feet.

"Essix!" Rollan exclaimed, and crouched beside her. The falcon was wrapped entirely in sticky spiderweb. She shrieked, outraged.

A skittering sound came from the forest all around them.

Meilin caught a glimpse of something moving through the branches.

No, not *something*. Lots of things—spiders, *thousands* of spiders. They were led by one spider larger than the others, which moved with uncanny intelligence.

In a flash, she realized what was happening. "One of the Oathbound has a spider spirit animal!" she shouted. And it had called other spiders to help it spin webs to entrap them.

"Run!" Abeke yelled.

Rollan scooped the entangled Essix into his arms and sprinted past Meilin.

Meilin started to follow when she heard a shriek from behind and turned to see Abeke wrapped in web, struggling to get free. Conor was frantically ripping at webbing that had covered his feet, holding him in place.

A second later, Meilin felt something—a mouse-sized spider crawling up the back of her neck. More spiders leaped at her from the trees, trailing threads of sticky web. As she went to draw her sword, another web, as wide as a net, drifted down from the trees, covering all five of the Greencloaks. They fought as it settled over them, but the harder they struggled, the more tangled they became, until they could barely move. Spiders crawled all over them, as if checking to be sure they were really caught. Meilin shuddered as a spider walked right over her face.

"Now I know what a fly feels like," Rollan gasped as he tried to protect Essix's feathers from the web.

When they were completely trapped and all five of them had fallen to the ground in one squirming, web-covered lump, Meilin saw dark shapes emerging from the trees. They were dressed in black, with the distinctive brass collars and wrist-guards. One of them was unusually tall and thin, with parchment-pale skin and deep-set eyes. Gripping his bony shoulder with huge talons was a hunched, black-feathered bird with a cruelly hooked beak and a wrinkled red head.

"That's Wikam the Just," Meilin heard Anka whisper. "One of the Oathbound's leaders. His spirit animal is a vulture, and it's a lot more dangerous than it looks. Listen," she went on quickly, "Wikam is not to be trifled with. His name might be *Just*, but he *will not* treat you fairly. Don't even bother trying to argue with him."

"I suppose you mean me," Rollan muttered.

"Shhhh," Anka hissed, sounding worried.

One of the other Oathbound gave a signal, and the swarm of spiders skittered off into the forest—except for one spider, his spirit animal, which scurried up his body to perch on his shoulder. The spider was small, brown, and furry—and really, Meilin had to admit to herself, nothing at all like a mouse. The moonlight glinted from its many-faceted eyes.

Wikam the Just folded his long arms and looked them over. "Well, well, well," he said in a deep voice that sounded like it was speaking to them from the other end of a cavern. "Look at you wiggle, little Greencloaks. But we've got you now. You *will* face your punishment for attacking the leaders of Erdas."

"But we didn't do it!" Meilin protested.

"You know something?" Wikam sneered. "I actually believe you." The Oathbound soldier leaned casually against a tree, his eyes sparkling with cruel amusement. "I just don't care. You could be as innocent as . . . well, as children. I'm going to bring you in anyway, and earn the glory for your arrest. You'll be put on trial for assassinating the Emperor of Zhong. And when you are convicted—which you *will* be, after I reveal to the leaders that you confessed your heinous crimes to me—the penalty will be *death*."

THE TORCH

DURING THE FINAL BATTLE AGAINST THE WYRM, THE Redcloaks' polar ice fortress, the Place of Desolation, had been rendered uninhabitable. Its lava tubes and mysterious markings from the Hellans were all gone now.

Ever since then, Stead, who had taken over as the leader of the Redcloaks after Shane's death, had been looking for a new place to make their headquarters. After scouting a few likely locations, he had decided to build a high tower on a remote beach on the south coast of Eura. Anybody who climbed to its very top could look out over the ocean and see the Greencloaks' castle on the island of Greenhaven, way in the distance.

Yes, Worthy had been up there. He was pretty sure that Stead's choice of a new location, and its view of Greenhaven, meant something. The Redcloaks were outcasts, and Stead wanted back in.

Well, *that* wasn't going to happen, Worthy felt sure. All any of them needed to do was look into a mirror to know why.

And yeah, he wanted in, too, though at the same time he rather liked his slit-pupiled golden eyes, not to mention the muscles he'd put on since he and his black panther spirit animal had merged. The retractable claws were good, too.

Still, Worthy saw Stead's point. Every one of the Redcloaks had made mistakes. Their late, great leader, Shane, had given them a reason for being–to redeem themselves. And according to Stead, despite their honorable fight against the Wyrm, they weren't done yet.

Stead stood on the wide, sandy beach, watching the workers he had hired putting a few last touches on the tower. It was built of sand-colored stone, with a roof of hammered copper that glowed flame-bright in the setting sun. It was so bright that anybody standing on the walls of Greenhaven and looking in this direction could probably see it, shining like a torch across the water.

Maybe that was the point.

"Hey, I know what you should name the tower," Worthy suggested. "The Torch."

Stead didn't answer. He looked all heroic, with his mask in place and his red cloak curling around his legs in the sharp breeze off the ocean. Waves crashed against the sand, and seabirds circled overhead. At Stead's feet, Yumaris squatted, picking with gnarled fingers through a pile of seaweed and shells that smelled like dead fish. She couldn't see what she was doing–she was more worm than human, really–but she sniffed at the sand and nibbled at the seaweed and seemed perfectly content.

Unlike Worthy. He sighed loudly, waiting for Stead to tell him why he'd been summoned. But Stead was becoming more and more like the spirit animal that was now part of him–as stubborn and hardheaded as a ram.

As if sensing Worthy's impatience, Stead looked over at him. Worthy caught a glimpse through the mask of Stead's odd, rectangular pupils.

"I've had some reports," Stead began.

Here we go, Worthy thought. He folded his arms and prepared to listen.

"The leaders of the four lands have come out of hiding," Stead said. "A few days ago, they gathered for a meeting at the old Citadel, on the border of Eura and Zhong."

"Yep!" Yumaris put in happily.

Worthy glanced down at the eyeless old woman. She was knotting bits of shell into her long, gray-white hair. Grinning with her toothless mouth, she draped a long scarf of seaweed over her shoulders.

"Very nice," Worthy said to her.

In response, she cackled and then threw a handful of sand in his general direction.

Stead went on. "The reports say that something went wrong at the meeting. The Greencloaks attacked the leaders, an act of terrible betrayal. The Ambassador from Stetriol was wounded, and the Emperor of Zhong was killed."

Wait, what? "The *Greencloaks* did this?" Worthy interrupted.

"Of course not," Stead said impatiently. "According to my sources, the attackers had only recently joined the Greencloaks. Clearly they joined intending to carry out the attack. And now the leaders of Erdas are convinced that all Greencloaks are criminals. They have ordered their Oathbound to track down and arrest every single Greencloak left out in the world." He pointed toward the island of Greenhaven. "Once they're captured, they'll be brought to their castle and imprisoned, and then they will all be put on trial."

Worthy felt a twinge of uneasiness. "So who set them up? Who wants to destroy the Greencloaks?"

Stead shrugged. "No idea. One of the leaders, perhaps? The Greencloaks have plenty of enemies, especially after so many of them fell to the Wyrm. They still have enemies in Stetriol, too, people who feel as Shane once did, that the Greencloaks were to blame for years of suffering by those who called spirit animals and didn't have the Nectar to ease the formation of the bond. So you see, Worthy, it could be anyone. Even a fellow Greencloak gone rogue."

"Or a Redcloak?" Worthy suggested.

"No," Stead said flatly. "Definitely not."

Worthy shrugged. As far as he could see, anybody was capable of anything. He wouldn't count out one of the Redcloaks until he was absolutely certain. "So what do you want me to do?"

Stead nodded. "Our favorite group of young Greencloaks managed to escape the Citadel without being captured."

Worthy felt his uneasiness growing. "You mean Conor and the other three?"

"Yes, the Heroes of Erdas," Stead answered. "I want you to help them."

"But they hate me," Worthy protested. At least Conor did, and he had good reasons for it, too.

"Make them trust you," Stead countered.

Worthy shook his head. "They are *never* going to trust me." When Stead didn't comment, Worthy went on, "I mean it. Never. Not ever. You've picked the wrong person for this mission."

Behind his mask, Stead narrowed his eyes. "Think of it this way, Worthy: It's your chance to be the good guy. The rescuer."

Oh, Stead was good. He knew exactly what Worthy wanted—what he had always wanted, from before the time he'd failed to summon a spirit animal at his Nectar Ceremony. He wanted to be the hero. Like . . . well, like Conor, who had been his servant, who he had treated as badly as he could get away with. Conor, who had summoned one of the Great Beasts and had gone from being a shepherd to becoming one of the Four Heroes of Erdas. "What would I have to do?" Worthy asked.

"Find the kids," Stead answered. "They probably think they've escaped, and they're wrong about that. They need to know that the Oathbound are rounding up all the Greencloaks in the world. Tell them what you know about the gifts. Help them."

"I don't know anything about any gifts," Worthy said blankly.

"Yumaris says otherwise," Stead said. "But you're right, nobody knows much about them. The ancient Greencloaks had a nasty habit of wiping out any information they thought was too dangerous. The gifts have apparently been lost for many years. But it's time they were found." He pointed at Yumaris. "She had a vision of you and the gifts, and now she will tell you about them."

Worthy groaned. "She'll tell me all about the consistency of dirt particles, is what." He glared at Yumaris.

She grinned up at him. "Gifts!" she said happily. "Rock and claw! Circle! And that other thingie!"

"*Thingie,*" Worthy muttered. "So helpful. Thank you *so* much." Then he shrugged. He was a Redcloak, and

Stead was his leader, *and* maybe this was his chance to finally prove that he was *worthy* in more than just name.

And . . . *claw*. Hmm. He just might know something about that. "All right," Worthy agreed, nodding at Stead. "I'll do it. What will you be doing in the meantime?"

"The Oathbound serve the leaders of Erdas," Stead answered. "Their intentions are honorable, but they're wrong about the Greencloaks. They're being manipulated by someone else. Just in case, we're going to need a larger force. I'll be gathering the rest of the Redcloaks, so we're ready to protect the Greencloaks if we have to."

Worthy had to admit that it sounded like a good plan. "Fine." He sighed. "I'll go find the Four Heroes. And whether they trust me or not, I'll make sure they're not captured. And I'll help them with the rock, the claw, the circle, and . . ." He glared at Yumaris. "With the *other thingie.*"

11

NIGHTMARES

"I FEEL CLOSER TO YOU ALL THAN I'VE EVER FELT BEFORE," Rollan said in a muffled voice.

"Rollan, your elbow is in my face," Abeke complained.

"I would say that I'm sorry," he answered, "except that your knee is up my nose."

"Stop wiggling," Anka grumbled. "It's just making it worse."

All five of the Greencloaks lay in a heap on the pine-needled ground. They were wrapped tightly together in the sticky spiderweb.

Most of the Oathbound had gone to fetch a wagon to transport the captured Greencloaks back to the Citadel, leaving the Marked man with the spider spirit animal and one other Oathbound on guard.

"Conor," Meilin whispered. "See if you can reach the knife on Rollan's belt."

"All right," he whispered back, and groped with his hand. He felt the grip of the knife with the tips of his fingers, but he was too entangled in web to reach it. Anyway, one knife would not be enough to cut them free of the web.

There was only one way out of this. From where Conor lay, tightly bound up with the others, he could see both of the Oathbound a few paces away, leaning against a tree.

"Listen," Conor whispered. The three other kids and Anka fell silent. "We have to escape now, before Wikam the Just—"

"The *Un*just," Rollan interrupted.

"Right, Wikam the Unjust," Conor went on. "We have to escape before he gets back with the wagon. On the count of three, we'll all call our spirit animals at the same time and break out of this web."

"One," Meilin whispered.

"Two," Abeke added.

"*Three,*" Rollan shouted.

Jhi burst from the passive state, tearing through the web that wrapped Meilin like it was tissue paper.

At the same moment, Uraza leaped forth, and her sharp claws shredded the web entangling Abeke.

And Briggan snarled, ripping the web away from Conor, who rolled free and jumped to his feet, pulling out his ax, ready to fight.

The Oathbound guards shouted; one of them drew her sword and the other snatched the spider from his shoulder and threw it at them. Sticky threads unfurled behind it, settling over Rollan, who was trying to struggle out of the net that had covered them before. Essix was still tangled, no help to him. Anka was fighting the web that covered her and her chameleon, too.

Drawing her sword, Meilin charged to meet the Oathbound guard, blocking her attack. Reversing the sword, Meilin struck with the pommel, knocking the guard unconscious; then she whirled and knelt beside Rollan, pulling the layers of web away from him. As they dried, the spider threads had become less sticky, but the kids all had rags of web clinging to them.

"Thank you, My Lady Panda," Rollan gasped as he finally broke free, still cradling Essix in his arms.

Abeke nocked her one remaining arrow and trained it on the Marked Oathbound, who stood with his hands raised in surrender. His spider had retreated into a pocket on the front of his uniform; Conor could see a brown, furry leg peeking out.

"Ugh, spiders," Rollan said, trying to free Essix's wing from the sticky threads without damaging her feathers. "One crawled right across my face." He shuddered.

"Just think of them as mice," Meilin advised him.

"Mice? Seriously?" Rollan shot back.

She gave him a smug nod. "That's what I do."

"I don't want a mouse walking over my face, either," Rollan muttered. In his arms, Essix shrieked out a protest at being trapped. "All right, I'll get you untangled," Rollan said to her. "Just hold still."

Finally, Anka freed herself from the last of the web. She had turned silvery white, like the strands that had covered her. "The rest of the Oathbound will be back soon," she said sharply as her skin, hair, and clothes darkened to match the color of the forest. "Let's get out of here."

They ran.

Conor had thought before that he was too tired go any farther. But as the sun came up, he found himself with the others, stumbling to a halt at the edge of a port town.

During the night they'd outdistanced their pursuers. Once they found a ship and left Eura and the Oathbound behind, they could begin their quest to find all four of the gifts. And he would be free to sleep.

Without nightmares, he hoped.

With Anka keeping them unnoticed, they slipped into the town, heading for the docks. There, Anka booked them passage on a ship bound for Amaya, paying the captain extra to finish loading their goods quickly, so they could catch the next tide. She hustled the kids onboard. They only had enough money for one cabin with two hammocks in it, so they would have to take turns sleeping.

They stood now, checking out their cabin. "The hammocks sort of remind me of spiderwebs," Rollan observed. "Creepy. I'm never going to fall asleep wrapped up in one of those things."

"Some of us aren't afraid of spiders," Meilin told him.

"Uh-huh," Rollan said skeptically.

As they took off their boots and weapons, he ran his fingers up the back of Meilin's neck. "Spider!" he warned.

She flinched and swatted, then turned red as she realized that she'd betrayed her fear.

"Mouse, I mean," Rollan teased.

Meilin folded her arms and glared at him.

"A cute, little, fluffy, brown mouse," Rollan went on, grinning, and Meilin gave in, laughing.

"You sleep first," Abeke said to Conor. She'd been keeping an eye on him, ever since their conversation in the Citadel. He remembered what she had said—that he was her truest friend. And what Olvan had warned as the stone viper venom had taken him—*stay true to each other.* Conor was determined to be as true and worthy a friend to Abeke as she was to him.

With a nod of thanks, Conor climbed wearily into the hammock, which swung to the side as the ship turned into the wind, heading out to sea. The one port-hole in their cabin showed the afternoon sun glinting on the surface of the water and the port town receding into the distance. They were safely away. The Oathbound would never catch them now. They'd have to go back to the Citadel and guard the leaders of Erdas, as was their duty.

Rollan had climbed into the other hammock. He'd spent the night running while trying to free Essix's feathers from the sticky spiderweb. Finally the falcon had stopped struggling and had gone into passive state, but Conor knew his friend was almost as tired as he was.

Uraza, who hated being at sea, was in passive state, and so was Briggan. Jhi had settled in a corner, filling a quarter of the cabin's space with her calm, healing presence. Meilin and Abeke sat on the deck, leaning back against the panda.

Anka was nowhere to be seen, but unless she moved, Conor tended to lose track of her. He figured she was in the cabin somewhere.

His hammock swung gently back and forth as the ship cut through the waves. Sleepily, Conor listened to Meilin and Abeke's quiet conversation as they shared out a meal of ship's biscuit and dried apples.

From the other hammock came the faint sound of Rollan, sound asleep, snoring.

"Rollan probably never had a bad dream in his life," Meilin said. Conor could hear the smile in her voice as she spoke about him.

"I bet he dreams about Tarik," he heard Abeke say.

"Yes, you're probably right," Meilin agreed.

There was a silent moment. "I have nightmares, too, once in a while," Abeke said softly.

"About what?" Meilin mumbled through a bite of biscuit.

Abeke's voice sounded sad. "Losing Uraza. And that moment when she attacked me. I was so afraid. Of her. If Shane hadn't stepped in, Uraza would have killed me."

"You're not afraid anymore, are you?" Meilin asked.

"No," Abeke said. "But I still think about it." Conor knew how hard it was for Abeke to be having this conversation without the comfort of Uraza's presence. But the big cat hated water; she was better off in passive state.

Meilin was quiet for a minute. "I know what it's like to doubt your bond with your spirit animal. You just have to trust."

"I do. I trust Uraza completely," Abeke said. There was a rustling sound. "I have a comb. Do you want me to unbraid your hair for you?"

As Meilin answered, Conor felt himself drift into sleep.

Where the Wyrm was waiting for him.

At first he was floating in a soft darkness, gently rocked by unseen waves. Then he looked down at himself. He was standing. At his feet, the darkness was moving. It was not soft or peaceful, he realized, and dread prickled over his skin. It was a seething mass of oily, black parasites. As he watched in horror, they flowed up, over his legs, their touch icy cold, until they covered his entire body. Then they pushed through his skin until he wasn't a boy anymore, just a boy-shaped collection of black, pulsing worms, with a piercing pain in his forehead where he'd worn the Wyrm's spiral mark. He opened his mouth to scream, and writhing black worms flowed out of him.

As his shout echoed in the tiny ship cabin, he jerked awake, then struggled out of the hammock, landing with a thump on the deck. He crouched there, shivering, still feeling the cold touch of the parasites.

The red light of sunset streamed through the porthole, turning everything in the cabin the color of blood.

And then Abeke was crouched at his side, taking his hand. "It's all right," she assured him.

"What's going on?" came Rollan's sleepy voice from the other hammock.

"Nothing," Meilin answered. Her hair was unbraided, a long, straight curtain of black silk that hung down her back. "Go back to sleep."

Conor kept shivering, still seeing the parasites. He reached up to rub his forehead, which ached.

"Look at me," Abeke said firmly, taking his chin in her hand. "You're all right." To his astonishment, she pushed his hand aside, leaned closer, and put her lips to the very spot where the Wyrm had marked him. After the kiss, she leaned back, and he stared into her wise, brown eyes.

"Let Jhi help," Meilin said, and moved aside so the big panda could come closer.

Jhi put a big paw on Conor's shoulder, and he felt the wet rasp of her tongue as it stroked over his brow, over the mark, over the place where Abeke had kissed him.

The constant pain of his forehead faded. The creeping dread of the Wyrm lifted.

A feeling of peace and healing spread through him.

Abeke nodded. "You're all right," she repeated.

"I'm all right," Conor agreed.

And suddenly, it was true. He let out a relieved breath. Even with everything that had happened, the terrible things he'd seen, the blood, the fighting, he wouldn't want to go back to being a simple shepherd. He was with his friends. He was where he belonged.

It had taken a long time. But thanks to his friends, he was finally, truly, free of the Wyrm.

12

PREY

"WE'RE BEING WATCHED," ABEKE SAID, STOPPING IN THE middle of the road. She'd been feeling prickly for the past hour, and she was a hunter—she knew when to listen to her instincts. At her side, Uraza crouched, her long tail twitching.

"But we left the Oathbound behind in Eura," Conor responded.

"Maybe we did," Abeke said, looking around alertly. "But we're still being watched. Followed. Stalked, maybe."

On reaching Amaya they had left the ship, and now they had almost reached Concorba. The dirt path they were on ran straight toward the city, through a forest crowded with trees that Abeke didn't know the names of, their leaves turning autumn colors—bright yellow, brown, flaming orange.

And . . . red. She caught a glimpse of something red disappearing behind a nearby tree. But it wasn't a leaf.

"I was right," Abeke whispered. "There's someone here."

"Should I hide us?" Anka asked. She hadn't taken on the colors of the forest, but her features seemed blurred. Somehow it was hard to get a really good look at her.

"No," Meilin decided. She put her hand on the pommel of her sword. She raised her voice. "Whoever is following us should show himself."

The only move from the forest was the rustling of leaves in a cool breeze.

At Abeke's side, Uraza's keen, violet eyes gleamed. Briggan stood beside Conor, his ears pricked, his big nose sniffing. Jhi was in passive state, and Essix floated high above the forest on a current of warm air.

"Behind that tree over there," Rollan said, pointing to where Abeke had glimpsed the bit of red.

Abeke grinned suddenly, feeling the thrill of the hunt. "Go get him, Uraza." At her words, the big leopard sprang forward. She leaped once, bounded around a tree, and pounced. There was a yell and a scuffle of leaves. The kids and Briggan raced after her.

As they came around the tree, they found a boy in a white mask and red cloak sprawled on the ground with Uraza's front paws on his chest. Uraza flexed her claws, and the boy yowled and squirmed, but she didn't let him up.

Red cloak. Cat mask.

"Worthy," Meilin said, sounding disgusted.

"*Un*worthy is more like it," Rollan put in.

"What are you doing sneaking around here?" Meilin demanded.

"I wasn't sneaking," Worthy protested.

"Following, then," Abeke said. "Stalking. Watching."

"All right," Worthy said, giving up. "Get this overgrown house cat off me, and I'll tell you."

It was a good time to stop to eat lunch, so the four kids pulled bread and cheese out of their one pack and sat on the leafy ground. They introduced Worthy to Anka, who nodded and then did her usual fade-into-the-background thing. Abeke, with her honed hunter skills, knew where Anka was, but all she could see, even looking straight at her, was a faint outline against the trunk of a tree. She wondered if Anka's skin only looked like tree bark, or if it had taken on that nubbled, rough texture, too.

"All right, *Un*worthy," Meilin said, pointing at him with the knife she was using to cut a piece of cheese. "Talk."

Abeke saw the Redcloak's strange slitted eyes blink behind his mask. "Our leader, Stead, sent me to warn you."

"Uh-huh," Rollan said skeptically. "Warn us about what?"

"The Greencloaks are officially being broken up." Ignoring their gasps, he went on. "The leaders of Erdas have ordered the Oathbound to arrest every Greencloak in the world," Worthy answered. "You are *all* to be put on trial for what happened at the Citadel."

"But we had nothing to do with the attack," Meilin protested.

"*I* know that," Worthy said. "All the Redcloaks know it. But to the rest of the world, you are renegades. You're to be arrested on sight. The Oathbound know you are here. They're tracking you. Stead sent me to warn you— and to help you."

The four Greencloaks looked at each other in dismayed silence. They had thought they'd escaped, but they were in much greater danger than they'd realized.

"Maybe we should abandon our quest for the four gifts," Meilin said slowly. "What Worthy is talking about—the suspicion, the arrests, the trial. It means the true end of the Greencloaks. Maybe we should try to figure out who is behind it all."

Abeke saw the logic of this. She saw Rollan and Conor considering it, too.

"No," came a voice from the edge of their clearing. Slowly Anka's form took shape as she stepped away from the tree where she'd been sitting. "The quest for the four gifts is far more important than you realize. You *must* find them. And isn't it the task that Olvan assigned you?"

"That's true," Meilin said. "It is. But still, I think—"

"Consider this," Anka said, stepping forward. Somehow her face was still in shadow, blurred, so Abeke couldn't get a good look at it. "The two tasks are connected. The gifts, once you've found them all, can be used to remind the leaders that the Greencloaks have always served the four lands of Erdas."

Abeke saw her point. "I think Anka's right, and we should continue," she said. "We should do as Olvan ordered. We should go on with the quest for the four gifts." She looked around the circle of her friends, and they all nodded agreement.

"I can help with that," Worthy said. "I know about your quest. I can help you find the rock, the claw, the circle, and the . . . uh . . . the other thing. And I can help you escape the Oathbound."

"Are you saying you want to join us?" Rollan asked skeptically.

"No way," Conor interrupted. "Have you forgotten who he really is? Devin Trunswick. He's a bully, and a liar, and he betrayed all of Trunswick when he joined Zerif."

"I was having a bad day," Worthy mumbled.

"He drank the Bile," Conor went on.

"I drank the Bile, too," Meilin reminded him.

"Not on purpose," Conor countered. "Not like he did. Who knows what else he's capable of? We can't let him join us."

As Rollan was nodding agreement, Abeke was shaking her head, setting her braids swinging. This kind of anger—it wasn't like Conor. She knew he didn't like Worthy; Devin Trunswick had treated him badly when he'd been the older boy's servant. Clearly the usually very forgiving Conor had not forgiven him yet.

She tried to reason with him. "But Worthy fought the Wyrm, just as we did," she said. And she couldn't forget that he was a Redcloak—just like Shane. No matter what else he had done, Shane had died a hero's death.

"And he seems to know more about the gifts than we do," Meilin put in.

"Not much more," Abeke noted, wondering where Worthy had gotten his information about the *rock, claw, circle, and other thing.*

"I really do want to help," Worthy said, sounding intentionally pitiful, Abeke thought.

The four Greencloaks exchanged a look. Rollan raised his eyebrows. Then Meilin nodded, and so did Abeke. Conor shot Worthy a look of deep dislike, and then he shrugged. "Maybe," he said reluctantly.

"We can give him a trial period," Meilin said, with a nod. "If he really is helpful, he can stay; if he's not, he'll have to leave. Agreed?"

All the kids nodded, and Worthy sighed loudly, as if they were being stupid for not accepting him immediately.

Abeke vowed to keep an eye on him, just in case. She accepted a piece of cheese on stale bread that Meilin handed her, sharing pieces with Uraza, who snapped them up and made a contented rumbling sound in her chest.

Abeke chewed a bite of bread, thinking. "You said the Oathbound are tracking us?" she asked Worthy.

He was looking longingly at the bread. He nodded, then pointed with his chin in the direction of Concorba. "They're probably lying in wait for you. They're not sure where you're going, but they expect you to pass through the city. That's where they'll capture you."

"We have to go into Concorba for supplies," Anka said, from just outside their circle.

As she spoke, Worthy jerked in surprise. "Yipes! I forgot you were there."

"Happens a lot," Anka said acidly. And, Abeke thought, a little sadly.

"Anka is right," Meilin said, holding up the heel of the loaf of bread and a rind of cheese. "This is the last of our food." After hesitating, she held it out to Worthy, who seized it and started eating, tearing off pieces and stuffing them under the mask, into his mouth.

Abeke stared at Anka, who was fading back into the color of the tree she was leaning against.

The Oathbound were tracking them. She realized that she needed to stop thinking like a hunter, and start thinking like the hunter's prey. It meant becoming more like Anka—passing through the land unnoticed.

"The Oathbound are hunting Greencloaks," Abeke said slowly.

"That's what he said," Rollan mumbled through a bite of bread, nodding at Worthy.

"Meilin, take out the gift," Abeke ordered. When her friend had taken out the rock and unwrapped it, Abeke pointed to it. "The rock is hidden. Unrevealed, as Olvan said. We have to be the same way. As the Heroes of Erdas, we're too easy to track. We have to go in disguise. We can't be Greencloaks anymore."

AMBUSH

ROLLAN GULPED DOWN HIS BITE OF BREAD AND CHEESE and jumped up. "No," he said forcefully. "Greencloaks are who we *are*. We can't take off our cloaks."

They all got to their feet, staring at him.

Rollan felt a red flush creeping up his face. "I know, I know. I was the last of the four of us to become a Greencloak. But look"—he pointed in the direction of Concorba—"I spent a lot of time hiding in that city, trying not to get caught by the militia. I didn't like sneaking around then, and I don't like the thought of it now. And remember what Tarik told us? He said we should never take off our cloaks. He said, *We must stand behind who we are and what we represent.* Remember? We should keep wearing our cloaks, and just be more careful."

"What's the problem, Rollan?" Worthy put in with a shrug. "Your cloak is basically rags. You should throw it away anyway, and get a new one when this is all over."

Worthy's comment hit Rollan like a punch in the stomach.

"Shut up, Unworthy," Conor said, glaring. At his side, Briggan growled, sensing the sudden tension in the air.

"What?" Worthy said, raising his hands as if surrendering. "What did I say?"

"This," Rollan said in a shaking voice, holding up the ragged edge of Tarik's cloak, "was given to me by a man who was braver and more *worthy* than you will ever be."

Worthy's face was hidden behind his mask, so it was hard to see how he was really feeling. But he took a step back and lowered his head.

Rollan clenched his fists. He wasn't particularly good at fighting. He usually managed to talk himself out of tricky situations. But if Worthy so much as opened his mouth, Rollan was going to punch him. Surprisingly, the Redcloak stayed quiet.

It was Meilin who spoke. "Rollan," she said softly, "I know you don't want to set Tarik's cloak aside. But Abeke is right. We take too great a risk being Greencloaks at a time when the Oathbound are hunting us."

"If they really *are* hunting us," Rollan shot back. He pointed at Worthy. "We only have his word for it that they are."

"We can't take the chance," Abeke said. "And remember, we *have* taken our cloaks off before."

Rollan remembered. He, Conor, and Abeke, along with Finn and the other Greencloaks, had been in Stetriol on what they had thought would be a suicide mission. It had been a matter of life and death. This situation wasn't so dire.

"We don't have any choice," Meilin said. Giving Rollan a sympathetic look, she unpinned her cloak and rolled it into a lump. "It's not safe to carry them with us," she continued. "If we really are fugitives, there's going to be a bounty for our capture. People will be watchful.

We might even have our packs searched. We can't hold on to any liabilities."

Then she stepped to the edge of clearing and dug a small hole with her sword. She kneeled there, tucking the bundle reverently into the earth. Abeke, Conor, and Anka followed one by one, each relinquishing their cloaks to the soil.

Maybe they were right. Slowly Rollan took off his tattered cloak. As he folded it carefully, Essix dove toward their clearing. She banked, circling him once and brushing his face with a wing tip, then settled onto his shoulder, a heavy weight. His cloak had a patch of leather sewn onto the shoulder so she wouldn't shred it when she perched there. Without it, her sharp talons pierced his shirt, like needles poking into his skin. She was not a comfortable passenger.

The falcon was not usually affectionate, but she bent her sleek head and ran the curve of her beak along the edge of his ear, comforting him. He reached up and stroked the dappled feathers on her chest, feeling better. Then he felt worse, realizing that if they were in disguise, their spirit animals would have to be hidden, too. He didn't look forward to convincing Essix to go into passive state again.

They decided that because Rollan knew Concorba best, he and Conor would go into the city to buy supplies. Meilin and Abeke would wait in the woods nearby, hidden by Anka, until they got back.

When Worthy insisted that he should go, too, Rollan and Conor ignored him.

"No, really," Worthy said. "I can carry the supplies."

When they didn't answer, he slumped, as if disappointed. "I just want to help, that's all."

Rollan heard Conor mutter something about *Unworthy*. It was a good name for the Redcloak. More appropriate than the one he had chosen, anyway.

Anka gave them a few coins, and Conor slung the pack for groceries over his shoulder. To Rollan's surprise, Essix went meekly into passive state; Conor had rolled down his shirtsleeves to cover the tattoo of Briggan on his arm. They set off toward Concorba, leaving their weapons behind, taking only the small knife that Rollan kept hidden in his boot. Being without his cloak made Rollan feel strangely defenseless, as if it were more than just cloth. As if it were a shield. To anyone seeing them, Rollan and Conor looked like two ordinary boys; specifically, Rollan looked like a rather scruffy kid from Concorba, and Conor looked like a slightly better-dressed Euran visitor.

They entered the city, keeping an eye out for the distinctive black uniforms of the Oathbound. They walked slowly, trying not to call attention to themselves. Rollan sniffed the air, smelling the familiar scents of roasted corn, pine smoke, horse dung, and drying chilies.

He glanced aside at his friend. When they'd first met up again on their journey to the Citadel, Conor had looked pale and unhappy, and though he wasn't the chattiest of kids, he'd been even quieter than usual. Rollan's ability to read people's moods had shown him how dark the other boy's thoughts had been. But Conor looked better now. "You having those dreams still?" Rollan asked.

Conor looked startled. "The Wyrm ones? No." He frowned down at his feet, thinking. "But last night I had another dream. About a wave."

Rollan flapped a hand at him. "That kind of wave?"

Conor laughed. "No, the watery kind."

"A prophetic dream?" Rollan asked.

"I'm not sure." Conor shrugged. "I'll let you know."

They kept to the side of the road, on a boarded side-walk, until they came to the store that Rollan knew belonged to Monte, a Greencloak they'd met when they had come to Amaya in search of Arax the Ram. Monte and his partner, Barlow, had run a trading post in Boulder City, a remote village. Barlow had been killed in a fight against the Conquerors, who had tried to take the Granite Ram talisman. Later in the war, Monte had fought with the Greencloaks against the Conquerors in Stetriol. When that battle had ended in victory, the man had returned to Amaya to set up a new store in Concorba.

Rollan had been looking forward to seeing bald, cheerful Monte, still telling jokes and selling supplies to travelers, but the front door of the store was locked, the windows shuttered.

"Won't find him here," a dry voice said.

Rollan and Conor turned to see an old man dressed all in brown rags sitting on the edge of the sidewalk, his bare feet in the dust of the road.

"Where is he?" Rollan asked.

"Well, now, let me think. Hmm." The old man held out a filthy hand, asking to be paid for the information.

With a sigh, Conor dug out some money—too much, Rollan noted—and gave it to him.

The old man eyed the coin. "Huh." He fixed the two boys with a bloodshot eye. "Monte's a friend of yours?"

"None of your business," Rollan said, before Conor could say anything. He knew his friend wasn't used to dealing with this kind of thing. "Where is he? Why is his shop closed up?"

The old man pursed his lips. "No need to get snippy, boy." Then he shrugged. "Some guard types came. Arrested Monte, took him away. A couple days ago, that was."

"Guard types," Conor repeated. "Dressed in black? Wearing brass collars?"

"Yep." The old man nodded enthusiastically. "Said they had orders from the Prime Minister of Amaya to arrest every Greencloak they could find. Would seem Monte is in big trouble." His rheumy eyes narrowed. "You wouldn't know nothing about Greencloaks, would you? There's a sweet reward out for information about them."

"No," Conor said hastily. "We don't know anything about Greencloaks. We've, uh, never even met a Greencloak." He gulped. "I'm not even sure we know what—"

"All right, thanks," Rollan interrupted quickly, seizing Conor's arm and pulling him toward the street before he could completely give them away. "Less is more, Conor," Rollan said as they hurried across the road. When Conor gave him a blank look, Rollan explained. "If you're lying, don't explain too much. It'll give you away every time."

"I know," Conor said, looking chagrined. "It just felt like he knew what we are. Do you think he suspected us?"

"Probably." Rollan looked back over his shoulder. There was no one sitting in front of Monte's store. Uh-oh. The old man *had* been suspicious, which meant he'd scurried away to tell somebody about the two boys asking after a Greencloak friend of theirs. It wouldn't take long before that information reached the Oathbound.

They had to hurry.

And Rollan had to admit that his friends—and Worthy—had been right. If they'd been wearing their cloaks, they would have been arrested already.

Moving fast, they found another store that sold supplies for traveling. The storekeeper seemed very curious, asking them where they were headed. When Conor started to answer truthfully, Rollan elbowed him in the side to silence him. He lied, saying they were heading for the coast to go fishing.

They came out of the store loaded with supplies—a full pack slung over each shoulder and their arms full. Staggering, they headed for the poorer section of the city. Dust swirled around their feet as they made their way down a narrow street, where the houses were little more than huts, and skinny dogs growled at them before skittering away.

Seeing a few familiar faces, Rollan nodded, returning their greetings. He'd grown up here, after all. People were bound to recognize him as one of the Heroes of Erdas. "This is not good," he said to Conor through clenched teeth. "A lot of these people know that I'm a Greencloak."

"Maybe we should get out of the city," Conor said worriedly.

"One more stop," Rollan said. "It won't take long."

"Where are we going?" Conor asked.

"Just down this street." A few months ago he'd gotten a letter from his mother describing what she'd been doing ever since the end of the Second Devourer War. "My mother opened a school. It should be just around this corner."

Conor blinked. He'd met Aidana, so Rollan knew how surprising this information was. "A school?"

"Yeah." Rollan took a few more steps, and then he stopped. "Look, you know that I was a street kid here for a long time. When my mom abandoned me, she did it because she couldn't take care of me. She had the bond sickness. She thought I'd be better off without her."

Conor nodded solemnly.

It was hard to talk about this stuff, but Rollan made himself go on. "I know she felt guilty about it for a long time." He pointed down the street toward a big building made of hard-packed adobe bricks. "She didn't get the chance to help me, so now she's trying to help other street kids. She opened up this free school." He shrugged. "Maybe they'll have some useful information."

"And you get a chance to see her," Conor said.

"Yeah, that too," Rollan admitted.

They dumped the heavy bags of supplies on a porch in front of the school. Just before they stepped inside, Rollan paused. "Go ahead. I just have to do something."

Conor nodded and went inside.

Quickly, Rollan dug into a small satchel at his side and pulled out his cloak. It had been less ragged and faded many months ago, when he and Tarik had been trapped by the Conquerors and only Rollan had been able to escape through a space too small for Tarik to fit into. As Tarik sent Rollan to safety, he'd smiled when his own green cloak settled over the boy. Shortly after Tarik's sacrifice, Rollan had taken his vows and had become a true Greencloak, united in purpose with his friends for the first time.

Rollan would never forget the pain of saying good-bye to the man who had become like a father to him. Even if he and his friends had to sneak around, he wouldn't leave Tarik's cloak behind. He stuffed it deep into the bottom of one of the sacks full of supplies. Then he followed Conor into the school.

As he stepped from the bright, sunny outdoors into the dimness of the schoolroom, all the students in the class stared at him. They sat on rows of benches, separated by a center aisle. Each kid held a notebook and pencil. Conor was already sitting down on one of the benches, as if he was one of the students.

And then Rollan saw his mother. She was standing at the front of the room, facing a wall painted black, writing some numbers with a piece of chalk. Her hair was a long black braid hanging straight down her back.

His mother, teaching math. He'd seen some strange things in his life, but this was possibly the strangest.

"*Pssst*," whispered a nearby kid. She poked his leg with a sharp finger. She was Niloan and had intricately braided hair and wore a sand-colored robe. "You better sit down, or you're going to be in trouble." She scooted over, giving Rollan room to sit on the bench beside her. "I'm Ngozi," she added.

"Your teacher's pretty tough?" Rollan whispered to Ngozi.

As she nodded, another girl, Amayan by the looks of her, leaned in and gave them both a stern look. "Our teacher," she said sharply, "is *wonderful*."

"Why's that?" Rollan asked, trying not to smile.

"I love, love, love math," she answered. "And Miss Aidana is a very good math teacher." This girl wore neat, colorful clothes and had long black hair, which, probably not by coincidence, she'd braided in the same style as his mother.

Ngozi rolled her eyes. "That's Sora."

"How did you find her school?" Rollan whispered.

"She found us," Ngozi began, "because we're—"

"*Shhhhhh*," Sora hissed, glaring. "We're not supposed to talk about that with"—she shot a knifelike glance at Rollan—"with *strangers*."

Rollan grinned, then saw his mother turn away from the blackboard, saying something about the math lesson. Her eyes rested on him and she froze. The chalk fell from her fingers.

"Ohhhh, you're in for it," Ngozi whispered.

Rollan's grin widened. "You have no idea," he whispered back.

"We've been studying numbers," his mother said loudly. "Specifically the number *one*."

"Here it comes," he said to Ngozi and Sora, and got to his feet.

His mother had her hands on her hips. "The number one," she repeated. "Which is how many letters my son has sent to me in the last three months."

All the kids were staring at him, wide-eyed.

Rollan couldn't stop smiling. "We were traveling," he told his mom.

She mock-glared at him. "No excuse." She opened her arms, and he went down the central aisle to the front of the room, where she pulled him into a hug. Then she set him back and looked him over, a hand on his shoulder. With the tip of a finger, she traced the scar on his face that he'd gotten during the battle against the Wyrm. "You've grown taller," she said softly.

She had a few more lines at the corners of her eyes. And she was even more beautiful than he remembered.

She cocked her head. "You said you were traveling." A smile hovered at the corner of her mouth. "With that darling girl, Meilin?"

Rollan felt a blush prickling on his face. "Mo-om!" he protested.

"Miss Aidana," shouted a tall, red-haired boy from the back of the room, interrupting them.

"Yes, Jean-Luc," his mother said, without looking away from Rollan's face.

"There's a bunch of people wearing black clothes outside," the boy said. "They have swords. And shiny collars."

Conor stood up from the bench where he'd been sitting. His eyes met Rollan's.

"Oathbound!" they said at the same time.

"You're in trouble?" Rollan's mother asked. Then she waved her hand. "Never mind. Of course you're in trouble. Need to escape?" At Rollan's nod, she pointed toward a door that opened from the back of the schoolroom. "Quick. This way."

Conor raced down the center aisle; Rollan met him at the door, which his mother flung open. It opened onto an alley. A figure dressed in black was coming from the right.

Rollan paused to give his mother a quick hug good-bye.

"Write to me," she said sternly, and pointed left. "That way. Run!"

Rollan and Conor went left, and the Oathbound came after them. They raced down the alley, bursting out into the area in front of the school with their pursuer on their heels.

Five more Oathbound were there, weapons drawn.

Frantically, Rollan glanced over his shoulder. The one from the alley was closing in from behind.

They were surrounded!

14

HERO

WORTHY GROANED.

Rollan and Conor. Greencloaks. Stupid. *So* stupid.

Of *course* the Oathbound knew about Rollan's mother's school. Even though Aidana wasn't a Greencloak, it was well known that her son was. But the two idiots, loaded with supplies, had walked right up to her front door in broad daylight.

At least Worthy'd had time to get the supplies hidden in a nearby alley before the Oathbound had shown up.

Worthy had been following Rollan and Conor since they'd entered the city, hardly noticing the odd looks from passersby. Ever since he'd taken up the mask of a Redcloak, ever since he'd woken up one morning unable to summon his spirit animal, Elda, he'd gotten used to stares. And then his eyes had changed, and his hands ached as retractable claws replaced his fingernails, and he grew sleepless with the prowling intensity of the big cat. His hair had turned sleek and dark...

...and really, nobody needed to know about the tail.

Now was his chance to prove to Conor and the others that he *was* worthy enough to join them. If only he hadn't made the stupid mistake about Rollan's cloak. Abeke had explained where he'd gone wrong, how Rollan had been a street kid who'd come to see Tarik as a kind of father—and how Tarik had been killed right in front of Rollan, leaving the boy holding his green cloak.

So yeah, he could see why it was important.

He'd make up for his mistake. He'd get them all to trust him.

At least Abeke was talking to him. She was a hunter, but she was wise and kind, too. Meeting her now as an ally, Worthy could see why Shane had been in love with her. Whether he'd admitted it to himself or not.

The beautiful, terrifying Meilin, though. He'd keep his distance from that one. She could probably take him apart with her little finger. Scary. Brrr.

He wasn't sure yet about the sharp, shy chameleon woman, Anka, though the Greencloaks seemed to trust her.

But for now, Worthy had to help the boys.

Crouching in an alley with the bags of supplies piled behind him, Worthy's panther-aided senses were on full alert. The six Oathbound rushed into the area in front of the school. Their leader gestured, and one of them broke off, circling around the back of the building.

An ambush.

Worthy heard a shout, and then Rollan and Conor raced around the corner of the school and stopped short, seeing the five Oathbound waiting for them; the sixth was coming from behind. Rollan pulled out what looked like a little knife from his boot. But it wouldn't be enough.

Good, Worthy thought.

The Oathbound closed in on the boys, brandishing their swords. Their leader, a tall, gaunt-faced man, was Marked. He had a huge black-feathered bird, a vulture maybe, riding on his shoulder.

Six adults, armed and well trained, versus two stupid kids who hadn't even called forth their spirit animals yet. Worthy waited another moment, just so they'd know how much danger they were in before he heroically rescued them. Before going, he checked that his long panther tail, which sometimes liked to wave free when he got into a fight, was hidden away. All set.

Just as the Marked Oathbound was about to grab Rollan, there was a flash of light, and Essix appeared in full flight, shrieking and slashing with her sharp talons at the face of the attacker, who fell back, wailing loudly. Essix arced higher to gain altitude for a strike against the vulture, which had launched itself awkwardly from its perch. Rollan leaned back to let an Oathbound woman's blade pass him by, then ducked and used a low kick to sweep her legs out from under her.

A move he'd learned from the terrifying Meilin, no doubt.

The woman scrambled away from Rollan, then got to her feet and fled down the street.

At the same moment, Conor called forth Briggan, who leaped from his arm, teeth bared, and knocked an attacking Oathbound to the ground; a quick bite to the shoulder and the man was writhing in the dust, moaning. Meanwhile, Conor caught the knife Rollan had tossed to him. He ducked a sword thrust from another one of the Oathbound.

What had been two versus six was already two versus three, and Conor was attacking, using the speed and agility he gained by Briggan being in his active state.

Whoops, Worthy thought. Better get in there and be a hero quick, before the Greencloak boys rescued themselves.

Feeling ridiculously gleeful, Worthy burst from his hiding place. One pantherlike leap, and he was close enough to the fight to rake his retractable claws down the arm of an Oathbound. Then he spun into a jump that took him behind the man Rollan was fighting. With a growl, he aimed a blow at the man's head. The Oathbound swayed before falling to the ground, landing with a thud. The man Conor had been fighting was trembling on the ground, with Briggan's big paws on his chest, holding him down.

Worthy, Conor, and Rollan had a moment to stand looking at each other as the dust of the fight settled around them.

Overhead, Essix soared and let out a fierce cry.

"More Oathbound coming!" Rollan gasped, blinking, and Worthy knew he'd been looking through the falcon's eyes.

The three whirled to see nine more black-clad figures charging down the street, led by the one who had run away. *Uh-oh*, Worthy realized. She hadn't been fleeing— she'd been fetching reinforcements.

Three against ten was another story. No, make that twelve—two members of the original Oathbound ambush were climbing from the ground, picking up the swords they'd dropped.

Rollan and Conor took up defensive stances, back-to-back. "Stay with us!" Rollan shouted at Worthy, as if *they* were going to protect *him*!

Both of the boys were panting. Conor gripped the small knife, their only weapon. Essix had landed on

Rollan's shoulder; Worthy saw the boy flinch as she caught her balance, her talons clinging to him. Briggan crouched at Conor's side, ready to attack.

Worthy formed up next to them. "What's the plan?" he asked.

"Uh, don't let them capture us?" Rollan said. He kept his eyes on the Oathbound, who were being ordered by the tall, thin Marked man with the vulture to split into groups. They'd attack from three sides.

"No plan," Conor said quickly. "We can't defeat that many. We'll have to fight our way free and run."

"Oathbound!" came the harsh call from the Marked leader. "Attack!" His vulture was perched on his shoulder. At his order, its ragged wings spread wide and it launched itself into the air, swooping closer as the black-clad soldiers drew their weapons—mostly swords, with just a few spears to keep things interesting.

Worthy extended his claws and crouched, ready to spring into action.

And then the Oathbound were on them.

Growling, Briggan leaped, tackling a soldier and sending his sword flying.

Overhead, the vulture, twice Essix's size, battled the falcon; the two birds clashed and then tumbled to the ground, trailing feathers. The vulture had no vocal cords, so it had no call, but it made a guttural hissing sound as it tried slashing Essix with its hooked beak. Worthy heard the falcon shriek with fury and saw her hurl herself into the air again, pursued by the ponderously flapping vulture.

Worthy lithely avoided the thrust of a spear and then bonked the Oathbound holding it on the head; the woman collapsed almost gracefully onto the ground.

Worthy then whirled in time to see Rollan fighting hand-to-hand with a man he must have disarmed; another Oathbound came at Rollan from the side, slashing the boy's arm with her sword. As Rollan flinched, the man he was fighting struck him hard in the face.

Rollan fell heavily to the ground, then rolled away from the fighting, shaking his head as if he was stunned. Blood spurted from the sword cut on his arm. He gripped it with his other hand, but blood leaked out between his fingers. "I'm out," he gasped, catching Worthy's eye.

And suddenly it wasn't about being a hero anymore.

Rollan was hurt.

Conor and Briggan were surrounded.

It was time to really fight.

Ripping off his mask, Worthy snarled out a challenge. For a moment, the Oathbound fell back before his rage—and at the sight of his slitted golden eyes and the claws that extended from the tips of his fingers. But at a shouted order from their leader, they seemed to take courage, gripping their weapons and surging back into an attack.

This is it, Worthy thought as he yowled and leaped to meet the onslaught. It didn't matter how well he fought—they were too many. Rollan and Conor were the ones they wanted; if Worthy ran, they probably wouldn't come after him. But he wasn't going to abandon the Greencloaks. He would do whatever he could.

Just as the Oathbound began their charge, the double doors to the school burst open, and three of the students, with Aidana, rushed out.

All three of the students were Marked!

Aidana flung out her arm, and her spirit animal, a raven, flashed into the air. With a harsh cry he joined

Essix in fighting the huge vulture. Aidana followed it into battle, going straight to crouch at her son's side. Whipping off an embroidered scarf, she wrapped it around his arm to stop the bleeding.

Meanwhile, her three Marked students had joined the battle. They were surprisingly skilled, Worthy could see at once. As he fought off the Oathbound leader, an Amayan girl called forth a flamingo, which flapped awkwardly into the air, joining the aerial battle among Rollan's falcon, his mother's raven, and the huge vulture. At the same time, a tall Euran boy drew a longsword and joined the fray. His spirit animal, a stag the same red as his hair, leaped past him and slashed at an Oathbound soldier with antlers as sharp as knives.

The third student was a Niloan girl. With calm and precision, she drew a throwing knife from the sleeve of her sand-colored robe, took aim, and hurled it toward one of the attackers. At her feet bounded a little gray fox with huge ears. Worthy heard it make a yipping sound— it was picking out targets for the Niloan girl's knives!

Clearly Rollan's mother was teaching more than just reading and math in her school. One day her students might become powerful Greencloaks.

The battle swirled around Worthy, and he fought with all his panther-given speed and skill. Even with the help of Aidana and the three students, it was only enough to give Worthy, Rollan, and Conor an opening to escape.

At the mouth of the alley Worthy had been hiding in before, Briggan gave a sharp bark, summoning them. "We have to run!" Worthy shouted.

"Yes, go!" Aidana struck with her staff. "Jean-Luc," she shouted at one of her students, "there's one behind you!" She whirled and yelled, "We'll hold them off. Run!"

Retreating, Rollan stumbled to the alley, Essix on his shoulder. A moment later, Conor joined him, calling for Briggan. Worthy snatched his mask from the dusty ground, then bounded into the alley, where he scooped up the bags of supplies. Handing one to Conor to carry, he followed as Briggan led them through a maze of winding alleys. The sounds of the battle in front of the school receded behind them.

"Left here," Rollan gasped. "Then straight on."

Oh, yeah, Worthy remembered. Rollan had grown up as a street kid in Concorba. He'd probably lived in these very alleys. A glance over his shoulder showed Worthy that Rollan had fallen a few steps behind. Sheathing his claws, he slowed and waited for him to catch up.

"We can rest a minute," Worthy said, putting down his load of supplies. His tail had been trying to escape; he tucked it quickly away before the two Greencloaks could see it.

Rollan nodded and leaned against a brick wall, breathing hard. He had a growing bruise on one high cheekbone, where the Oathbound had punched him. The scarf his mother had wrapped around his arm was stained with blood.

Conor turned back and set the bag he was carrying on the ground. A nod to Briggan, and the wolf flashed into his dormant state. "Better not to be noticed now," he said.

The three boys stood in the shadowy alley, catching their breaths. Worthy listened intently for sounds of pursuit but heard nothing. Just the everyday noises of a busy marketplace not far away, and a horse passing in a nearby street. "I think we're clear," he said quietly.

"For now," Rollan said. "But they'll be coming."

Worthy nodded in agreement.

"That was good, remembering the supplies," Conor said to him.

Worthy bent his head to tie on his mask, not wanting to reveal how pleased he was by Conor's comment. Maybe the ice between them was beginning to thaw. With his toe he shoved one of the bags closer to Rollan. "I knew I had to get that one." Mask in place, he looked up at the other boy but said nothing more.

He'd seen what Rollan had stored inside the bag.

Rollan just stared at him for a moment. Then he nodded. He glanced back the way they'd come. "I hope she's all right."

Ohhhhh. Worthy suddenly realized what he'd been unable to see before. Of *course* Rollan had known the Oathbound would be a danger, but he'd gone to see his mother anyway. He loved her. Just as he'd loved that Tarik guy.

Devin Trunswick had grown up with everything–family, a luxurious home, servants, and the knowledge that he would be an earl someday. And yet he'd still always hungered for more.

It was a hunger that had led him straight to the Conquerors.

When Devin eventually lost everything that he'd *thought* he wanted, he discovered what truly mattered to him. There was one person in his life who'd always love him, even when he made a mistake as big as joining an evil army. His brother, Dawson.

It was Dawson for whom Devin had finally decided to be Worthy.

Rollan, in contrast, had grown up with nothing, not even a family. The people he loved probably mattered more to him than anything.

Worthy swallowed. "I'm sorry about"—he flashed his eyes subtly toward the bag—"before."

Rollan nodded. "It's all right," he said briefly. He studied Worthy for another moment. Then his mouth quirked into half a grin. "You yowled during the fight, didn't you?" he said.

Worthy blinked. Was Rollan teasing him? "I didn't *yowl*," he protested.

"Yes, you did," Conor put in seriously.

"See?" Rollan said, as if he was being completely reasonable. "You howled, Worthy. Like a cat with its tail being pulled."

"Yowled, you said, not howled. And I never yowl," Worthy corrected. "Or howl." He waited a beat. "Though I have been known to caterwaul now and then." Then he realized that Rollan, for the first time, had called him by his chosen name. And even Conor had joined in the joke.

As he returned Rollan's grin, he realized that maybe, finally, he had proved himself worthy of it.

15

GLUE

"I NEED MORE ARROWS," ABEKE SAID. AT HER SIDE, URAZA stood and stretched, then resettled in a patch of sunlight. Her violet eyes dropped shut as she dozed off again.

"We need more everything." Meilin lifted her sword and inspected the blade, newly sharpened. Light glinted off the polished metal. Sheathing the weapon, she got to her feet. "Rollan and Conor should have been back with the supplies by now." And Worthy. The Redcloak had spoken briefly with Abeke, and then he'd disappeared. Following the boys into Concorba, she assumed. *Helping*, he probably thought of it.

And speaking of disappearing . . . Meilin glanced around the clearing they'd been waiting in.

There, a movement, and she caught a glimpse of Anka's outline, blending into the rough brown bark of the tree she was leaning against.

So far, the Greencloak woman had been a valuable asset. But Meilin had long ago stopped thinking of people only as resources to be used. Maybe Anka could be a friend, too.

Meilin stretched, then ran through a few simple fighting forms, just to limber up. Then she paused. "Anka, would you like to spar with me?"

"No," came the brusque answer. "I don't fight. I hide."

Nodding, Meilin stepped closer, then crouched near where she thought Anka was sitting. "Would you put your chameleon into passive state?" she asked. "I'd like to see what you really look like."

There was a moment of silence. Meilin knew that Abeke was listening, too. "Nobody sees me as I am," Anka finally said. The usual sharpness was missing from her voice.

"Sometimes," Meilin said, "you don't have to hide."

"I would like to see you, too," Abeke put in.

"All right," the Greencloak woman said softly. There was a flash as the chameleon went into the dormant state.

Meilin saw Anka take shape before her. The woman sat very still—she must have trained herself to move as little as possible, in order to stay hidden. Revealed, Anka wore her green cloak. She sat cross-legged, her arms folded. The mark of her chameleon was wrapped around her wrist like a bracelet. Her hair was black and bristly, cut very short. Her eyes were dark brown, her face plain and ordinary, and . . .

"You're from Zhong!" Meilin exclaimed, delighted.

"You noticed," Anka said dryly.

"I would have noticed before, if you'd let me," Meilin said. And now she knew another reason why Anka didn't know how to fight—in Zhong, girls weren't supposed to study the martial arts. "Let me teach you a few forms, Anka," she insisted, getting to her feet.

"You never know when you might need to fight." She took up a basic stance, standing very still; then she made a quick strike at the air and returned to her stance. "See? You could hit somebody out of nowhere. They'd never see you coming. Come and try it."

"If you insist," Anka said, standing up, but Meilin could see that she was interested.

They spent an hour this way: Meilin teaching, Anka awkward at first but learning quickly. Meilin was showing her where to strike an opponent's neck to incapacitate him or her, when Uraza lifted her head and pricked her ears, alert. The tip of her spotted tail twitched.

Meilin heard it next—the sound of leaves crunching underfoot. Someone was coming, and not being too stealthy about it. Abeke got to her feet, raising her bow and nocking her single arrow.

Then Meilin relaxed. Coming through the trees were the three boys, carrying bags of supplies.

Her eyes went straight to Rollan. His face was bruised, and she saw with alarm that he was wearing a makeshift bandage. It was stained with blood.

"Can I get some panda spit here?" he asked, holding up his arm. He smiled to show her that he was essentially all right.

"Trouble?" Abeke asked.

Conor nodded and dropped the bags he'd been carrying onto the leafy ground. "Worthy was right—"

"You hear that?" Worthy interrupted, grinning. "Me. I was right." He thumped himself proudly on the chest.

Conor stared at him for a long moment, then gave his head a rueful shake. "Anyway. The Oathbound were on the lookout for us. Wikam the Just was leading them." Kneeling, Conor was unwrapping another bundle that he'd been carrying. He handed it to Abeke. "Arrows."

"Ah, thank you!" Abeke said, seizing them and inspecting each arrow. She'd want to be sure they were made well and would fly straight.

Rollan settled on the ground and started trying to untie the bandage around his arm with one hand. "We had a little scuffle."

"It was hardly little," Worthy said. He'd taken up a position at the edge of the clearing, looking back in the direction they'd come. "We've only got a couple of minutes. The Oathbound will be on our tail soon. Our trail, I mean."

Something had changed, Meilin realized. She knelt beside Rollan and carefully unwrapped the scarf from around his arm. The boys were treating Worthy as if he was . . . well . . . a friend. Even Conor was looking at him without frowning, and Meilin knew that Conor had very good reasons for hating Devin Trunswick. Clearly Worthy had proved himself in that little *scuffle* they'd had. It must have been quite a fight.

As Meilin took off Rollan's bandage, she saw that he had a gash on his arm about as long as her hand. It wasn't too deep, but it oozed blood, and she knew it had to hurt. With a quick gesture she summoned Jhi from passive state. The big panda yawned and rubbed at her eyes sleepily.

Rollan held up his arm. "Give me the spit, bear," he said. Jhi sniffed at it, then licked it three times with her pink tongue.

Meilin saw Rollan relax. Yes, it had been painful. Now at least it wouldn't hurt as much, and there wouldn't be any danger of infection. Meilin didn't have time to stitch it up, but hopefully there was a field medical kit in the supplies and she could see to it properly later.

Suddenly Anka was at her shoulder. As soon as the boys had returned, she had called her chameleon spirit animal and faded once again into the background. "Conor said Wikam the Just was leading the Oathbound. We need to go."

From his lookout spot, Worthy nodded. "Yeah." He nodded at Rollan. "You all right?"

"Fine," Rollan said, and pulled his sleeve down over the scarf that Meilin had finished retying over his wound.

Conor and Abeke each picked up a bag of supplies. Meilin, Anka, Rollan, and Worthy did the same.

"Let's go," Anka said, and they headed out.

By traveling hard and sleeping light, and never kindling a campfire, they managed to remain ahead of the Oathbound scouts who hunted them.

All six of them had faced such hardships before. Their spirit animals helped them; they knew how to cross the land without leaving a trace. But they were still in danger from a scout who searched for them from above.

Every now and then Rollan caught sight of Wikam the Just's vulture floating in wide circles over the land, its ragged wings catching every warm updraft, its keen eyes in its featherless red skull searching, always searching. Whenever Essix gave a warning cry, Anka had the four Greencloaks and Worthy freeze where they stood, and she camouflaged them until the huge bird had passed.

Every evening, Rollan sent Essix aloft to check on their pursuers. He would close his eyes, unsteady on his feet until he blinked and opened his eyes again.

"Still on our trail," he reported every night.

Relentless.

The Oathbound were relentless.

The Greencloaks, with Anka in the lead and Worthy bringing up the rear, were crossing a land of bare, weathered red rocks that the wind had twisted into odd, bulbous shapes.

Rollan was walking two steps ahead of Meilin. He closed his eyes and suddenly tripped, sprawling onto the stony ground.

"*Ow*," he mumbled. He scrambled to his feet, looking up at the cloudless sky. "Essix is to the south. The vulture is coming."

Anka, who looked reddish and weathered like the rocks they were crossing, hissed out what sounded like a curse. "Hurry." She pointed at a shelf of rock with a shady spot below it. "There."

Quickly they put their spirit animals into dormant state and shoved their bags of supplies into the hiding place, then squeezed themselves in so the shadow of the rock overhead covered them. Anka went still, and they all turned the same lined, red shade of the rocks.

The air was dusty, and it tickled in Meilin's nose, but she didn't dare sneeze. She was sitting next to Rollan, with Abeke on her other side. They waited in a heavy silence for a few minutes.

"Anything?" Anka whispered to Rollan.

There was a pause while he looked at the land through Essix's eyes. "It's still circling," he reported.

They were silent. Meilin felt the hardness of the stone beneath her. She wished she could shift to a more comfortable position, but that would give them away to the bird that hunted them.

After a few more quiet minutes, Conor asked a question, hardly moving his lips. "I've been thinking. What if the leaders of Erdas and the Oathbound *do* break up the Greencloaks? What will happen?"

They all considered it. Meilin knew that, while the Oathbound were a threat, the real enemy was whoever had sent the Fakecloaks, as Rollan had called them, to attack the meeting in the Citadel. That mysterious person or group was the true enemy—*they* had tricked the leaders of Erdas into thinking the Greencloaks were assassins. They were using the leaders and the Oathbound for their own purposes. Breaking up the Greencloaks might be only part of their plans.

A moment later, Meilin heard Abeke's soft voice. "Do you remember our Greencloak vow?"

Rollan answered immediately. "Yes."

"*Shhhh,*" interrupted Anka.

Rollan went on in a whisper. "Our vow is a lifetime commitment to stand united with the Greencloaks and defend Erdas."

"Exactly," Abeke said. "United. It's like what Olvan said when he sent us on this mission."

"We have to stay true to each other, he said," Conor put in.

"Not only that," Abeke went on. "We Greencloaks are . . ." She paused. "I don't know how to describe it. We're like the glue that keeps all of Erdas from falling apart."

"Glue, seriously?" whispered Rollan.

Meilin heard Worthy snort out a laugh.

"Can you all please shut up?" Anka hissed in a whisper. "Or at least don't move for the next ten minutes? Unless," she added acidly, "you actually *want* that vulture to see us."

As she spoke, Meilin saw the shadow of the great vulture cross the sunlit rock just beyond their hiding place. She stilled, trying not to breathe.

And she remembered what the emperor had said to her—that the Marked of Zhong should *belong* to Zhong. He had seen her not as a person, not as Meilin, daughter of General Teng, but as an *asset* and a *resource*. "If we were just Marked," she whispered slowly, "and not Greencloaks, eventually our countries would use us as weapons."

"But there's no war," Conor whispered.

"There would be," Worthy put in, his voice sardonic.

Meilin didn't nod, but she agreed. Without the Greencloaks to keep the peace, the great countries of Erdas would fracture. Everything would fall apart.

"We would have to fight each other," Conor said, and Meilin could hear the horror in his voice.

She felt it, too. Fight against Abeke? Against Conor? Against *Rollan*? No. Never.

But what if none of them were given any choice?

Abeke's voice was the barest whisper. "It's up to us. There is some force that's trying to disband the Greencloaks. It will try to divide us from each other. In the same way, it wants to divide the great nations of Erdas from each other. But we have to fight it. Together. The gifts will help, starting with the Heart of the Land. And so will our friendship. *We* are all of Erdas, united."

At Abeke's words, Meilin felt goose bumps prickle over the skin of her arms. She had always admired her friend's wisdom, but Abeke had spoken a deeper truth. They faced a mysterious force that had already killed the Emperor of Zhong, and now it was going after the Greencloaks. It would try to divide them. To destroy the Greencloaks forever. After that, there would be chaos. War. Death.

There was a long, awed silence.

"So you're saying we really do have to be glue," Rollan whispered. "I guess that means we're stuck with each other." Meilin could hear the strain in his voice. He was trying to lighten a heavy moment.

Moving slowly, Meilin edged her hand over the cool, lined rock until her fingers touched his.

Yes, Rollan, she thought. *We're stuck.*

SNEAK ATTACK

THE NEXT MORNING THEY LEFT THE STONE LANDS, moving into a rocky, forested area thick with pine trees and loud with waterfalls. Rollan remembered passing through land like this before, on his first mission with the Greencloaks—before he'd actually *been* a Greencloak. They'd followed Conor's vision of Arax, trying to find the Granite Ram talisman. In this part of Amaya, the air was dry and cold, and the sky was a deep blue without a single cloud.

The lake with the island called the Heart of the Land was not far away, Anka told them. They only had to stay ahead of Wikam the Unjust and his Oathbound trackers for a few more days, and they would be there.

And then, they all hoped, they would figure out how to *reveal* the rock.

Rollan still wasn't sure what that meant, exactly. The night before, Meilin had brought the rock out again, had unwrapped it, and they'd gathered to look at it.

"So what're you supposed to do with it?" Worthy had asked.

"Reveal it," Meilin had told him.

Then he'd reached out, grabbed the rock, and started picking at the scales that seemed to cover it.

"Stop that!" Meilin said. "You'll break it."

Worthy had dropped the rock on the ground, then bent to pick it up again. "It's a rock. It's not going to break."

At that, Meilin had snatched the rock away from him, wrapped it up, and turned her back on Worthy.

The masked boy shrugged. "I was only trying to help."

After a day of hard travel, they set up a rough camp at the side of a stream that rushed loudly through mossy stones. They ate a cold dinner of travel biscuits, jerky, and dried apples. Anka, of course, was not to be seen. Conor sat quietly talking to Abeke, Briggan close to his side. Uraza was at the edge of their camp, on guard. Worthy sat on a fallen log, throwing bits of twig into the stream.

Jhi, who was not the best traveler, had been dormant all day. With a flash of light, Meilin called her out. The panda's black eye-spots made her face seem almost mournful as she looked around the meager campsite; then she lumbered to a nearby tree and started stripping it of its brown, late-autumn leaves.

"Not her favorite," Rollan said. His arm barely hurt anymore, and didn't need any more Jhi spit. He still had a smudge of a bruise, a sore spot over his cheekbone, another reminder of their fight.

"She'd rather have bamboo," Meilin acknowledged.

Rollan pointed upstream. "Essix saw a waterfall up that way," he said to Meilin. "Want to take a look?"

Meilin set aside the sword she'd been sharpening obsessively and got to her feet.

Worthy turned his slitted pupils on them. "Where are you going, Rollan and Meilin?" He grinned. "Reilin, I mean."

Looking over at Meilin, Rollan saw that her face had turned bright red. He knew he was blushing, too. For once, he didn't have a sarcastic answer ready. Instead, he just glared at Worthy.

Worthy laughed—until Meilin turned her own glare on him. "Yipes!" Worthy said, and fell off the log he'd been sitting on.

Rollan stalked out of the camp, heading upstream. Meilin followed him, leaving Jhi to her dinner.

Reilin. Ridiculous!

They went along the stream in awkward silence, climbing over mossy rocks, winding around ferns and pine trees, until they came to the pebbly bank of a pool. The fresh, clear water stood at the base of a waterfall, which poured from a notch in a cliff high above. The falling water hitting the pool was so loud, Rollan could feel it in his bones.

The air was colder here, and a chilly mist from the waterfall drifted over them. Meilin shivered, and Rollan stepped closer. In silence they watched the swags of white water pour down, turn to lace, and then slam into the pool at the base of the cliff. Rollan had never seen anything so beautiful in his life.

He moved even closer to Meilin, speaking right into her ear so she could hear him over the roar of the waterfall. She had droplets of water in her braided hair, shining like pearls. "I remember something Tarik once told me," Rollan said. "He said, *I want to know Erdas in all her different forms of beauty.* And so do I."

Meilin nodded, her face still and serious. "Erdas would be less beautiful if it was divided, or at war."

Rollan looked down, because meeting her eyes would be too intense. "I can't imagine having to fight you, Lady Panda."

"For one thing," Meilin said, smiling, "you'd lose."

Rollan laughed. *That* was true.

And then, a smile still on her lips, Meilin leaned closer.

They had kissed each other once before, but it had been during a moment of excitement and happiness, and it had lasted about two seconds. Maybe less. Was she . . . Were they going to kiss again?

Rollan felt half afraid, half excited, and half . . .

Wait, that was too many halfs.

Shut up, he told himself, and, leaning toward Meilin, he closed his eyes.

A shrill scream pierced the air, even louder than the booming roar of the waterfall.

Rollan jerked away from Meilin. His eyes popped open.

There were sounds of shouting and yowling—Worthy—the roar of a big cat—Uraza—and then the clash of weapons.

"The camp," Meilin gasped. "It must be under attack."

As one, they turned and raced toward the others, dodging trees, skidding over the mossy rocks. The sun was close to setting—it was hard to see where they were going.

Meilin reached camp first, Rollan half a step behind her. Their friends were in the thick of a battle, one they were already losing. The shadowy forest around their campsite was swarming with Oathbound fighters, who darted and hid between the trees, not venturing into the clearing, but flinging knives, shooting arrows, and hurling spears.

Briggan was a gray blur as he leaped on the nearest Oathbound and bore her, screaming, to the ground.

Conor had pulled out his ax, but he had nobody to use it on—the Oathbound attackers kept striking briefly and then melting back into the darkening forest.

There was a scream from among the trees—Uraza was out there, stealthily hunting, a swift and deadly shadow.

A thrown spear had pinned Worthy's crimson cloak to the log he'd been sitting on; he was frantically trying to get the cloak off so he could stand up and fight.

Abeke had just finished stringing her bow. From his place on the edge of the camp, Rollan saw an Oathbound aim an arrow at her.

"Abeke!" he shouted. "Look out!"

The enemy arrow streaked across the camp. Calmly, Abeke looked up, and with leopardlike speed, snatched the arrow out of the air, flipped it, nocked it on her bowstring, and fired it back in the direction it had come from. Rollan heard a cry as it struck the Oathbound archer.

Meanwhile, another Oathbound was venturing into the camp with a spear ready, approaching Conor from behind.

Rollan drew his long knife and opened his mouth to yell a warning to his friend, when Anka struck the spearman from nowhere, a focused blow to the face. Then she disappeared again, and the spearman dropped to the ground, blood fountaining from his nose.

"Did you teach her that?" Rollan asked Meilin.

"Duck!" she shouted.

He didn't question that kind of order. He hit the dirt, and Meilin aimed a swift blow where his head had been, knocking the swooping vulture out of the air. The bird flopped to the ground, then awkwardly flapped its wings to get airborne again.

Climbing to his feet, Rollan heard Essix's outraged shriek—the falcon *really* hated the vulture. Using the speed of his bond with the bird, Rollan swooped into the clearing. His dagger blocked a knife thrown by a shadowy figure, who now darted behind a tree. "There!" he shouted to Essix, and the falcon dived down to claw at the knife-thrower's eyes.

Finally freeing his red cloak, Worthy jumped up from the log, his curled fingers bristling with his retractable claws. Seeing that the Oathbound were hiding among the trees, he yowled in frustration. "Cowards!" he shouted at them.

But even more Oathbound were coming. The air was thick with arrows that, somehow, didn't quite seem to hit their targets—Rollan thought they probably had Anka's chameleon power to thank for that. A dagger flashed past his face and embedded itself in a tree behind him.

"There are too many!" Meilin shouted as she fought against three shadowy figures at the edge of the camp.

"We have to retreat," Anka ordered. She was a blur of night-black and green. "Come on!"

"But the supplies!" Worthy protested.

"Leave them!" Anka ordered.

Meilin disarmed one opponent, ducked a spear thrust from another, and raced to follow Anka. Conor and Briggan followed, as did Worthy.

Rollan started after them, then took a quick detour to grab the pack containing Tarik's cloak. An arrow hit the pack as he slung it over his shoulder; he raced past Abeke, who was backing out of the clearing, keeping an arrow nocked, covering their retreat. Uraza bounded past her, and she turned and ran.

The five Greencloaks and Worthy fled from the camp, past the waterfall, and kept going farther upstream until they had left their attackers behind. Panting, they stopped in a clearing, where they stood knee-deep in ferns. The sun was just setting, and the dim and dusty light of evening had settled over the forest. In half an hour, it would be fully dark.

Rollan saw Conor cock his head, listening, his hearing acute thanks to his bond with Briggan. "They're not coming."

"We're clear—for now," Abeke agreed.

Rollan pulled out the arrow that had hit the pack and handed it to her; she nodded and added it to her quiver. He was aware of Essix perched on a nearby branch, settling her feathers after her fight with Wikam the Just's vulture.

"Is everyone all right?" Meilin asked, inspecting her sword, wiping it clean on her trousers, then sheathing it. She looked around to see everyone nod.

Rollan frowned. "Why did they let us go?"

"We were too mighty?" Worthy said with a shrug. "We fought too fiercely?"

Rollan gave him a look that said, *You are such an idiot.*

"I mean it," Worthy protested. "Did you see that thing Abeke did, catching the arrow?" He mimed drawing back a string and firing a bow. "It was amazing!"

"Yeah," Rollan agreed. "But the Oathbound outnumbered us five to one."

"They definitely could have taken us," Meilin put in.

Rollan knew she was right. Then he let out a breath, realizing what was happening. "They haven't been hunting us. They've been driving us." He glanced at

Abeke, the best hunter in their group, and she nodded, agreeing. *"Oh,"* Rollan went on. "They don't want us."

"What do you mean?" Worthy asked. "They're hunting and arresting all the Greencloaks they can find."

"They might want us," Rollan clarified, "eventually. But what they want first is the rock. The gift. Wikam the Unjust must know about the Heart of the Land."

Meilin nodded, understanding. "I think you're right. They'll wait for us to reveal the rock, and then they'll try to take it from us."

"We can't let that happen," Conor said seriously.

"Maybe we should split up," Abeke said. "Conor and I could lead them astray while Meilin and Rollan head for the island in the lake."

"And me," Worthy said.

"No," Meilin said. "I know we've had to split up on other missions, but on this one we can't. It's like what Rollan said: We're glue. We have to stick together."

"We have to stay true," Conor added, "like Olvan said."

Anka stepped out of the shadows; her features were blurred, hard to read. "Make up your minds. What are we doing?"

"We can't turn back," Meilin said. "Somehow, the four gifts are the key to saving the Greencloaks."

"And maybe more than that," Abeke put in.

"So we head for the lake," Meilin said, "and once the rock is revealed, we'll figure out how to evade the Oathbound trackers. Anka can help us with her chameleon powers. Agreed?"

The others, including Anka, nodded.

"Can we rest here tonight?" Worthy asked.

"It depends on how close the trackers are," Meilin answered. "Rollan, can you take a look?"

With a nod, Rollan called up to Essix; he could see her amber eyes watching him from a high branch in a nearby tree. With a rush of wind, she launched herself into the air, swooping high, flapping her wings to gain height.

Rollan closed his eyes, felt the usual dizzying rush of darkness and wind, and then saw a falcon's view of the forest. From this high, the sky was pinkish-gray to the west where the sun had gone down, and deep blue-black to the east where the night was rising. The waterfall was a strip of lacy white that almost glowed in the fading twilight; the stream was a shiny black ribbon running through the dark clouds of trees. Essix's keen gaze showed Rollan the Oathbound trackers in the Greencloaks' camp, going through the packs, tossing food and other supplies onto the ground. Wikam the Just watched them with arms folded, his bony shoulders hunched.

"They're searching for the rock," he said aloud, without opening his eyes.

He tried to count. The Oathbound wore black, so they were hard to see among the trees, but he thought there were about fifteen of them, including Wikam. A few had been wounded in the fight; they were being tended.

From the corner of Essix's eye Rollan saw a flash of black, and Wikam's vulture struck the falcon hard from the side—a sneak attack. His vision whirled as Essix tumbled, then steadied as she caught herself and banked and met the vulture's next attack head on. The two birds clashed together—Essix's talons tearing at the vulture's wrinkly red-skinned head and malevolent mud-brown eyes. Its hooked beak—made for disemboweling already-dead prey—ripped at the falcon. There was a spray of blood, and Essix released her talons and fell away. The vulture gave a harsh croak of victory.

The ground spun closer as the falcon plunged downward.

"Essix!" Rollan gasped, dizzy.

"What's going on?" he heard Meilin ask.

"Hold on a minute," he panted, and felt a hand on his shoulder, steadying him.

Come on, Essix—fly!

There was another terrifying moment of Essix plummeting from the sky. Then the falcon's wings caught the air, and her fall turned into a wobbly glide. Rollan spied the vulture, slower, flapping after her. She went higher, using her speed to stay ahead of the other bird.

As the falcon climbed even higher, Rollan realized what the vulture had been trying to prevent Essix from seeing.

With a gasp, he opened his eyes, blinking, then gazing around in horror at his friends, at Worthy, at the faded shadow that was Anka.

"It's not just trackers," he said. "Those are only scouts. There's a whole *army* of Oathbound out there. And they're coming after us."

17

HIGHNESS

AT THE DOOR WAITED THE LEADER OF THE CITADEL'S Oathbound guards, Brunhild the Merry. "Your Highness," she said, bowing.

Princess Song did not turn from the mirror. Her hair was smooth, intricately braided, secured with jeweled pins. Her face was heavily made up, her lips red, her eyes outlined in black, her dainty nose and cheeks dusted with rice powder.

"Your Highness," Brunhild repeated.

Song watched her own face. It was perfect. Unmoving, like ice.

The proper way to speak to a princess was to call her *Your Highness*. A ruler—an emperor, a king, or a queen—was addressed as *Your Majesty*.

It meant something, Song knew, that the leaders of the lands of Erdas still referred to her as *Highness* and not *Majesty*.

Her father, the emperor, was dead. Zhong *needed* an empress.

Lifting her chin, Song considered her own face. Every feature was perfect. It was the face of a *Highness*, but it was not majestic. Not as her father had been. People did not look to her for guidance. No, they thought *quiet* and *obedient* and *pretty*.

Song had told Meilin that she envied her, and it was true. Even without the careful makeup of a royal princess, Meilin was beautiful—as beautiful as a drawn sword. Meilin looked the way a true empress would look. Powerful. Skilled. Dangerous. Deadly.

Song knew she would never look like that.

In order to take her proper place—in order to help the people of Zhong—she would have to prove herself all those things.

"Your Highness," Brunhild repeated again from the door.

Song allowed one carefully penciled eyebrow to lift just a hair higher. It was an expression her father had made many times. In the mirror, she saw the Oathbound guard's reflection shift uncomfortably.

"Your Majesty," Brunhild corrected herself.

Song did not allow herself to smile. But she was satisfied.

She owned Brunhild's loyalty. The Oathbound was sworn to serve her. But she had a great deal of work to do before the leaders of Erdas would consider her an equal. And then, on returning to Zhong, she would have to convince an entire country of her ability to rule. To be *Majesty* instead of *Highness*.

Gracefully, Princess Song rose to her feet. "Have the leaders gathered?"

Brunhild bowed. "They have. They await you."

A regal nod, and Song led the way from the Zhongese wing to the Citadel's main meeting room.

The chamber in which her father had been killed.

By Greencloaks.

Despite an intensive search by the Oathbound, the four youngest Greencloaks had all escaped, leaving their comrades behind.

As Song stepped into the meeting chamber, her eyes went to the six-sided table that stood in the center of the room. Its surface had been scrubbed, but the stain of her father's blood remained, soaked deeply into the wood.

Sitting at the table was the Niloan High Chieftain, old and set in his ways. Next to him was the Euran Queen, who was always accompanied by a retinue of three or four nobles from her kingdom. She was young, very blond, and had oddly vacant eyes. The other leader was the Amayan Prime Minister, a middle-aged woman with a disapproving pout on her face. The Ambassador from Stetriol was there, too. She had been wounded in the same attack that had killed Song's father. Her arm was crooked in a sling and her skin was ashy pale. She should probably still be in bed, recovering.

Song circled the table until she reached the Emperor of Zhong's seat.

The last time the leaders had met, she had stood behind this chair, eyes lowered, until she had dared speak out, defending the Greencloaks.

Zhong must not appear weak to the other nations, even now. Especially now.

Decisively, she sat in the emperor's chair, folded her hands in her lap, and looked around the table at the other leaders.

They stared back at her. But none challenged her right to sit at the table with them. Song allowed herself a tiny moment of triumph. The rest of the meeting would be a challenge—her chance to begin proving herself as a true leader.

The Niloan High Chieftain cleared his throat and began. "Now that the *princess* has finally arrived," he said in a voice tinged with complaint, "we can decide what to do next about the Greencloaks."

"I'll tell you what we must do," said the Amayan Prime Minister sharply. "The Greencloaks must be broken up and returned to their own lands. Those who were involved in this disaster must be rooted out and prosecuted."

"The Greencloaks are bad" was the Euran Queen's contribution.

"*Bad* doesn't even begin to describe them," complained the Niloan High Chieftain. "They are corrupt. They serve only each other. They owe their proper leaders no allegiance. Clearly they cannot be trusted."

The queen looked around the table, blinking. "They cannot be trusted," she repeated.

Princess Song sighed inwardly. The Euran Queen was lovely, but there wasn't much going on behind her pretty blue eyes. "I advise patience," Song said.

"Patience," scoffed the Amayan Prime Minister. "There can be no doubt about the Greencloaks. The attack in this very chamber told us all we need to know about them."

"And yet they *have* served all the nations of Erdas," Song said.

"They served in order to gain power for themselves," the prime minister said. "And look where it has led!" She pointed at the bloodstain in the middle of the table. "Your own country, Zhong, has been left leaderless!"

Song took a steadying breath. Yes, she mourned her father. But now was a time for action, not tears. *She* would guide her people, if they'd only give her a chance. "As we all know," she said calmly, "Greencloaks all over the world are being arrested and arraigned."

"And when we catch them all, we'll put their traitorous leaders on trial—for murder!" shouted the Amayan Prime Minister.

"The Niloan Greencloaks must be returned to Nilo," the high chieftain put in, folding his skinny arms. "In my country we have harsh penalties for betrayers."

"They must be treated fairly," Song insisted. Carefully she caught the eye of the Euran Queen and gave an encouraging nod.

"They must be treated fairly," the queen repeated.

The ambassador had not yet spoken. Now she cleared her throat and said, "The world is watching us now." She nodded at Song. "Stetriol agrees with . . . with the daughter of the Emperor of Zhong. The Greencloaks must be gathered and sent to Greenhaven, where they can be imprisoned until they're given a trial—a *fair* trial."

"Did they give the emperor a fair trial before they killed him?" demanded the high chieftain. "They are assassins. Which one of us will they attack next?"

The meeting continued. Now Princess Song stayed quiet, observing how the leaders' tempers were fraying. There were signs of disunity. As the leaders argued, they didn't seem to realize what a danger that meant. Maybe they had been hidden away for too long to understand that leaders were supposed to *lead*. Not sit around arguing with each other. At one point, the Amayan Prime Minister banged her fist on the table and sourly told the Euran Queen to stay quiet unless she had something intelligent to say. In response, the queen's eyes filled with tears. Gathering her courtiers, she fled the room, weeping. The Niloan High Chieftain followed, snorting his disgust and stalking out.

As the meeting ended, Princess Song, followed by her Oathbound guards, headed for the Citadel tower where the two Greencloak leaders were still imprisoned. The rest of the Greencloaks captured in the Citadel had been sent ahead to Greenhaven, but these two remained for questioning.

At the tower, a guard bowed and opened the door. Princess Song entered the cell where the Greencloak leader was being held. The other one, Lenori, was next door, but it was Olvan who Song wanted to see.

Olvan had been bitten by Brunhild the Merry's spirit animal, a viper. The snake's venom had turned his body hard, like stone. Orders had been given that Olvan should be treated with just enough of the antidote to keep him alive, but not enough to allow him to move or to be a danger. He could only breathe, and blink.

The Greencloak leader was a big, gray-bearded old man with a stern face set in a fierce frown. Some of the guards must have lifted him out of bed, for Olvan was propped against one wall, as still as a sculpture.

Seeing Princess Song, he blinked. His lips twitched, as if he wanted to speak. But the venom had its hold on him, so he could not move any more than that.

"Greetings," Song said politely. "I expect you are worried about the four young Greencloaks. The Heroes of Erdas, as they're called."

Olvan blinked.

"They have not been captured. At last report, they fled to Amaya." Song stepped to the cell's window and looked out. "You have a nice view here of the mountains." She glanced at the old man, who could only stare straight ahead. "I don't suppose you've seen it, though, have you?"

She stepped into his line of sight. His face, she thought, grew sterner. Angry, even. She sighed softly. "Why Amaya?" she wondered. She gave her head a brief shake. "They cannot hope to escape. The Oathbound are everywhere."

She waited a moment, as if to allow him a chance to respond. When he remained silent, she went on. "Your Greencloaks are being gathered in Greenhaven. The castle is to become their prison. We thought it a small mercy to hold them in a familiar place until they can be put on trial."

As she continued, she lifted her chin, as if wrapping a cloak of *Majesty* around herself. She spoke as the Empress of Zhong would speak. "On trial for what, you may wonder? And I will tell you. You, Olvan, and all the Greencloaks, are charged with treason, and with the coldhearted murder of the Emperor of Zhong." For just a moment, she remembered the bloodstained table, and her voice wavered. "My f-father."

The Greencloak leader did nothing but stare straight ahead, without even blinking. It was as if he hadn't even heard her words.

18

THE WAVE

ABEKE HAD CHECKED HER ARROWS THE DAY BEFORE. As morning approached, she checked them again, looking them over one by one as she walked. The shafts were straight, that was the main thing. The feather fletchings were balanced. The tips were razor-sharp. These arrows would fly true.

They would need to. Rollan's report the night before had horrified all of them.

An army. An entire army of Oathbound soldiers, hundreds of them, with the relentless Wikam the Just as their leader. Abeke glanced at the sky, but she didn't see the vulture. She had tried shooting at the bird before, but it usually flew too high. Now she couldn't risk losing any arrows.

After hearing Rollan's report, Anka had led them through the forest, keeping them invisible so any Oathbound scouts would not be able to track them. They had no time to stop and rest for the night. The trail led uphill toward the lake where the island called Heart of the Land was located. If they went quickly and quietly, Anka said, they could reach the lake by early morning.

Just as the sky lightened with dawn, Anka let them rest for a few moments. While Abeke inspected her bow, Uraza flopped on the ground beside her. The others sat, and Worthy pawed through the one bag of supplies that Rollan had managed to rescue from their camp.

Worthy pulled something out of the pack and quickly handed it off to Rollan. Abeke didn't get a good look at the object.

Standing, Rollan yawned loudly, then he stepped away to stretch and get ready. When he returned, he was wearing an enormous brown cloak he'd picked up in town. It looked bulky and warm in the Amayan heat, but Abeke supposed he found the weight of it comforting, after giving up Tarik's cloak.

Worthy peered into the bag. "Nothing in here but medical supplies." He looked up, his eyes wide behind his mask. "Do you know what this *means*?"

"No," Conor said wearily. He sat with his back against a tree, Briggan's head on his leg. "What does it mean?"

"No breakfast," Worthy said sadly.

And no dinner, either, Abeke knew. She gritted her teeth and tried not to think about it.

"Let's go," Anka said. The sky was growing light. "It's not far now."

Groaning, they all got to their feet. Abeke saw Meilin pat the pouch where she kept the rock—the unrevealed Heart of the Land. Checking to be sure it was still there.

The path they followed wound between huge pine trees. It was studded with stones and crossed by twisted roots—Abeke had to watch where she was going, or she could easily fall. Uraza paced beside her, ears pricked, violet eyes watchful. Anka and Conor hiked a few steps ahead with Briggan. Meilin, Worthy, and Rollan came after.

"Did you hear that?" Worthy asked.

"What?" Meilin asked, stopping in her tracks and cocking her head. "Is it the Oathbound scouts?"

"No," Worthy said, sounding disgusted. "It was my stomach."

Uraza turned her head and growled at him.

"Yes, *growling*," Worthy complained. "I'm starving!"

"You've missed exactly one meal," Meilin said calmly, and started walking again. "You're hardly starving."

"I *am*," Worthy said dolefully, following. "Starving to death." Then he glanced over his shoulder at Rollan, who walked two steps behind him with Essix. The gyr-falcon had been slightly wounded in her fight against the vulture. She was now riding on Rollan's shoulder, looking ruffled and annoyed. "Rollan," Worthy said, "you're from Amaya. You must know how to forage for food. Tell us where to find roots and berries."

"Oh sure," Rollan said sharply. "If somebody threw roots and berries on a trash heap in Concorba, I'm your guy. That's the kind of foraging I know about."

"Cranky," complained Worthy.

Abeke couldn't stand another second of this. "Worthy, were you ever in your entire life unsure of where your next meal was coming from?"

"Not until now," Worthy answered grumpily.

"Oh, *poor* you," Abeke heard Rollan mutter, and he did sound a little cranky.

Abeke didn't blame him. They might have let Worthy join them, but the Redcloak boy was still intensely annoying. Some of the time.

They traveled as the morning continued, climbing higher and higher, until Abeke felt light-headed from hunger and the altitude.

Ever since the attack on their camp, there had not been a sign of the Oathbound, neither the trackers nor the army. Abeke thought it meant Rollan had been right the day before—Wikam the Just and his Oathbound knew about the rock and wanted the Greencloaks to *reveal* it before they pounced.

Well, she and her friends would be ready for them. Uraza was ready, for sure. Abeke had never seen the leopard so on edge, or Briggan, either. Both spirit animals were eager to fight.

There was a grumbling sound.

"Did you hear that?" Worthy said.

"*Stop* complaining about your stomach!" Meilin snapped.

"I'm not!" Worthy protested. Abeke turned to see him pointing at the sky. "Thunder," he said grimly.

He was right. Abeke had been watching the path, trying not to trip, and she hadn't noticed how the morning was getting darker instead of lighter. Now the clouds were gray, and so low they seemed to be snagged on the pointed tips of the pine trees. Distant thunder growled again.

Quickly, Abeke unstrung her bow and wrapped it in its leather case. The string couldn't get too wet, or it wouldn't function when she needed it. She wrapped the arrows in the quiver, too.

"No, Worthy," she heard Meilin say, a little scornfully, "we are not stopping to shelter from the storm. We have to go on."

There was more grumbling. Worthy, this time, and not the thunder.

Abeke smiled to herself. She suspected this was more than just Devin Trunswick's fussiness showing through.

As a Redcloak, Worthy had taken on aspects of his spirit animal, the black panther.

Conor stepped up to walk at her side. "What are you smiling about?" he asked.

She shrugged. "Worthy. He's like Uraza—like most cats. He doesn't like getting wet."

Conor glanced down at Briggan, who trotted at his side with his tongue lolling. "We don't mind the rain." Then he nodded toward Rollan, who was coming up the rutted path behind them. "But I bet we're all going to wish for our old cloaks by the time today is over."

Perhaps Rollan had been wise to replace his after all. Abeke agreed, and they went on. A few spatters of rain began to fall, heavy drops that made little craters in the dusty path.

"Abeke," Conor said, in a low voice, "speaking of getting wet . . ."

She nodded to show him that she was listening.

"Four nights ago I had a dream," he said.

She glanced quickly at him. "Not a—"

"No," he reassured her. "Not a Wyrm nightmare. I'm done with those. Something else." He swallowed and looked away. "Almost as scary."

Abeke stopped short and called to the others to join them. They gathered on the path in a tight circle.

"What's the matter?" Meilin asked.

"Conor must have grown faint from hunger," Worthy said.

All five of the Greencloaks scowled at him.

"Sor-*ry*," Worthy said, rolling his eyes.

"Conor had a dream," Abeke explained. As she spoke, the wind from the coming storm grew stronger. The pine branches in the forest all around them trembled, and the air turned sharply colder. Thunder rumbled in the sky, closer than it had been before.

Rollan glanced up at the gray clouds. "Ominous," he said.

"You had a prophetic dream?" Meilin asked, all business.

Conor nodded. "I think so. I've had it twice now, so I figure I'd better tell you about it, just in case." He looked around the group. "I was standing in a high place. The first time I had the dream, I couldn't tell where I was. The second time, I could see that I was standing on a stone surface, maybe the tower of a castle or a cliff. At the beginning of the dream, everything is dark. Then a light comes up, and I'm looking over the surface of an ocean."

His blue eyes seemed to be seeing that sight again, Abeke thought. They had a faraway look.

"The ocean is completely flat," Conor went on. "It's creepy. Too quiet. I stand there for a long time, and then I notice that the water is pulling away." He shook his head. "Or like it's taking a deep breath. Then the noise starts." Above them, the thunder grumbled, and Conor jerked with surprise. "Like that. Like thunder, but without stopping. I'm still looking out at the ocean, and I see a shadow in the distance. It grows taller and taller, rising from the surface of the water, as tall as a mountain, until it blots out the light, and then I see that it's a wave. A huge wall of water rushing toward me." He swallowed.

Abeke was staring at him; so were the others, their mouths open, their eyes wide.

"And then what happens?" Anka asked dryly.

Conor took a deep breath. "The wave leans over, and the top of it turns white with foam as it crests." He shook his head. "I can't do anything. I just stand there and watch it as it arches overhead. It's roaring, thundering. My heart is pounding, but I can't move. And then it crashes down over me."

"Let me guess," Worthy put in. "Then you wake up."

Meilin turned a fierce glare on him. He made a noise that sounded like *meep* and backed away.

But Conor was nodding. "Yes, then I wake up."

To Abeke's surprise, Anka had put her spirit animal, the chameleon, into passive state. She stood there, unhidden. Her face was pale, and she had deep shadows under her eyes. "Come with me," she said, without her usual sharpness. "I want you to see something."

They followed as Anka led them up the steepest, rockiest part of the path yet. The trees grew closer together, too. With the clouds like a low ceiling overhead, it was almost like being in a dim cave, Abeke thought.

And then, suddenly, the path grew level. Four more steps, and they came out of the forest to stand on the pebbled shore of a lake so wide they couldn't see the other side of it.

In the middle of the lake was an island.

"Is that it?" Anka asked in a subdued voice, pointing. "Is that what you saw in your dream?"

As one, they all turned to Conor to see what he would say.

19

STORM

RESTING HIS HAND ON BRIGGAN'S ROUGH-FURRED HEAD, Conor gazed out at the island in the middle of the lake.

He had expected the Heart of the Land to look like a regular island. Like a low hump in the middle of the lake, with trees growing on it.

This island was nothing like that.

It was like a huge, square pillar jutting out of the water. There was a thin ribbon of beach around its base, where waves lapped, but then it went straight up—all gray, rocky cliff face—until it ended in a flat top. It was taller than the tallest castle tower Conor had ever seen, and from where they stood on the shore of the lake, its steep sides looked impossible to climb.

But that's where they had to go to reveal the rock that shared its name with this island—the Heart of the Land.

"Is it?" Rollan interrupted.

Conor blinked. "What?"

"Is that the place you were standing in your dream?" Meilin said, pointing at the island.

Conor frowned and studied it. "I don't know." His dream had been so dark. "I'm pretty sure it was an ocean, not a lake."

"Water, though," Rollan pointed out, "and a high place."

"It *could* be," Conor said slowly. He looked around at his friends, and at Worthy and Anka. "It doesn't matter if it is or not. We still have to go out there, right?"

"No way," Worthy said quickly.

"Shut up, Worthy," Rollan and Abeke said at the same time. They grinned at each other, then quickly turned somber again, knowing how much danger they were about to put themselves in.

"No, seriously," Worthy said, putting his hands on his hips. "I mean, *look* at the island. It's not even an island! It's made out of cliffs! And we don't have a boat, so we can't get out there. *You* can't, I mean, because I'm not going. And then you'll have to climb to the top of it in the middle of a storm. And now there's this wave thing that Conor dreamed about that might be coming? You'd have to be crazy to try it."

"So anyway," Rollan said, ignoring Worthy, "I'll send Essix out to take a look around."

"We need to hurry," Meilin reminded him. "The Oathbound will know we're here, and they'll be coming."

Rollan nodded, then turned and whispered something to Essix on his shoulder. After a moment, Essix launched into the air. With a shrill cry, she swooped higher, buffeted by the gusts of wind that were coming in ahead of the storm. Steadying herself, she flew straight toward the island.

Rollan closed his eyes and he frowned, concentrating. Conor knew he was seeing through Essix's eyes.

"As much as I hate to admit it, Worthy's not wrong," Rollan muttered. Conor could only barely see Essix in the distance, circling the island. "This thing *is* all cliffs.

But there might be a way up. There's a flat area at the top, and a big rock shaped like a crescent moon. Huh. I thought there might be an arrow with a sign saying 'Reveal the Heart of the Land here.'" He opened his eyes again. "But there's not."

"It doesn't sound too promising," Abeke said.

Rollan shrugged. "We still have to try to get up there."

"You can't *climb* the island," Worthy put in, "because you can't even *get* to the island."

Rollan raised his eyebrows. "Essix showed me a way out there." He pointed with his chin along the curve of the lake. "Over that way is a long strip of sand that leads out to the island. Sort of like a bridge."

"It's probably not sand," Worthy said glumly. "I bet it's quicksand."

All four Greencloak kids glared at him.

"I know, I know," Worthy muttered. "*Shut up, Worthy.* But I'm not wrong. This is a completely terrible idea."

It was hard to admit, but as he stood at the end of the sand path, Conor thought Worthy might be right—again.

What Rollan had called a *bridge* was a thin line of sand winding in an S shape from the pebbly shore toward the pillar-like island. The clouds overhead were roiling, and growing darker by the minute. Thunder growled, and lightning flashed on the distant horizon. The lake's waves were whipped by the wind, washing over the narrow strip of sand. They'd be lucky to make it out to the island.

Meilin had decided that Anka and Worthy should wait on the lakeshore to keep an eye out for the Oathbound army, and to prevent them from crossing the sand bridge if they decided to come after the Greencloaks.

"That doesn't sound like a very rewarding task," Worthy complained.

"You could come with us, Worthy," Meilin said, and she gave him a sweet smile.

He flinched. "No, that's all right. You go ahead." Then he added under his breath, "And try not to kill yourselves while you're at it, all right?"

To Conor's surprise, he found himself stepping closer to Worthy. "She gave you a dangerous task," he said. It was hard to read the face behind the white mask, but Conor thought Worthy was worried. "We're counting on you."

"I'll do my best," the other boy said. Then he added in a rush, "And . . . and I'm sorry for the way I treated you, Conor. You know, back in Trunswick, and the rest of it."

"You were having a bad day?" Conor asked.

He saw Worthy gulp. "Ha-ha," he chuckled awkwardly. "Yes. A bad year. A bad everything. But I'm trying to be better."

Conor was silent for a long moment. "Before the Wyrm, I might have thought that anyone who did the things you did was beyond saving. But . . ." He shook his head soberly. "When the Wyrm took me, I did bad things. And I thought for a while that it made me a bad person. But it didn't. I am worthy. And maybe, so are you."

He saw Worthy's slitted eyes blinking rapidly behind his mask. Then he whispered, his voice shaking, "I hope so."

Conor put a reassuring hand on the Redcloak boy's shoulder. "I'm sure you will be."

As thunder rumbled and the storm prowled closer, the four Greencloaks set off across the sand bridge. The sand was soft underfoot and shifted at every step. Waves washed across their feet. Across the choppy water, the island loomed closer as they struggled along the narrow bridge of sand. Uraza led the way, leaping from one dryish spot to the next, clearly unhappy about getting her paws wet. Abeke followed, her strides long and powerful thanks to her bond with the leopard. Then came Meilin, followed by Rollan, then Briggan, with Conor bringing up the rear, bounding with wolflike confidence.

At a distance, the island's cliffs had seemed unscalable, like slick stone walls. But as they grew closer, Conor saw that the cliffs were covered with fissures and ledges. Even so, it still looked difficult to climb. Each wall sloped gradually outward; the top of the island was bigger than the bottom.

Ahead of Conor, Essix whirled past on a gust of wind. The blast had them all fighting to keep their feet on the sandy path. Then she banked and landed awkwardly on Rollan's shoulder, flapping her wings to steady herself.

"She can't fly in this storm!" Rollan shouted. His brown cloak whipped in the wind. Its shadowed inner lining almost looked green under the stormy sky.

Conor nodded, and they went on.

The thunder grew louder. Conor saw fingers of lightning probing the lake. The clouds lowered until it was almost as dark as twilight, and the wind gusted. Ahead, Conor saw Meilin stumble. He yelled out a warning, and Rollan grabbed her arm before she could tumble into the freezing lake water.

At last they trudged from the path to the narrow strip of rocky shore at the base of the island. At the same moment, the clouds opened, and an icy rain pelted down.

They gathered into a tight group. Uraza looked wet and miserable, and Briggan's tail was lowered, raindrops dripping from his fur.

"What now?" Abeke shouted to be heard above the wind and the pounding rain.

Rollan wiped the rain off his face and pointed. "There's the way up," he shouted.

At first, Conor only saw the dark gray cliffs looming overhead, streaming with water. Then he saw what Rollan was talking about.

All down the cliff face ran a narrow rock tube like a chimney, about two feet across. Water gushed down it. It was a waterfall, running from the top of the island to the bottom. They were supposed to climb up this way?

Conor glanced at Rollan, who nodded.

He knew what Worthy would have to say about this: *You're all completely crazy.*

The spirit animals would not be able to make this climb. Uraza and Briggan, and even Essix, joined Jhi in passive state.

Thunder crashed overhead, and they started up the cliff. First Rollan, who as a street kid had climbed the roofs of Concorba, evading bullies and the town militia. Then Meilin, then Abeke, and Conor last.

Rollan climbed a few feet and then shouted down at them, "There are handholds! Somebody's come this way before!"

Conor followed, finding it was true, though the handholds were covered with slippery moss and slick from the rain. The thin stream of the waterfall rushed past his right shoulder. As he climbed, he fell into a rhythm. When Abeke's booted foot left one tiny shelf of rock, Conor put a hand there and pulled himself up. The rock was gritty under his fingers, which were growing numb with cold. But the chimney of rock protected them from the worst of the wind.

Halfway up the cliff, there was a ledge just a few inches wide, a resting place. Rollan waited there for the rest of them to catch up. The four kids clung to the gray rock face, trying to catch their breaths as the wind battered their backs.

Conor looked over his shoulder, then closed his eyes, dizzy.

"Don't look down!" Rollan shouted from close beside him.

But Conor had already seen the tiny strip of beach where they'd started their climb . . .

. . . and from this height, the lake surface seemed smooth. Just like in his dream. Turning his head, he looked toward the horizon, half expecting to see the huge wave. If it was coming, it would crash into the island and wash them all off the cliff and into the lake.

Instead he saw the worst of the storm bearing down on them. The boiling clouds were a sickly greenish-black and flashed with continuous lightning. Thunder boomed overhead, loud enough to shake the island.

All four of them cringed against the cliff face, holding on for dear life. Rain lashed down. The howling wind pried at their fingers as if it wanted to whirl them away to their deaths.

"We have to keep going!" Conor heard Meilin shout.

Conor opened his eyes and nodded. Following the others, he edged toward the next handhold, and suddenly his foot slipped from the edge. The sickening feeling of falling flashed through him—and then Abeke's hand grabbed his arm.

"Hold on!" she yelled, steadying him.

It reminded him of the time he'd been having a prophetic dream at Greenhaven Castle and had sleep-walked right off the edge of a tower. Essix had snagged his cloak in her talons long enough for Abeke to grasp his arms and pull him up. Ever since then he'd been a little queasy about heights.

Abeke remembered, too. "Steady on!" she said, with a reassuring nod. She started climbing again. Conor took a deep breath, then followed. Blinking the rain out of his eyes, he looked up just as a clap of thunder broke right over the island. The rain turned abruptly colder, and every handhold became instantly crusted with ice. Lightning flashed, blindingly bright. In its aftermath, Conor saw Rollan, who was still leading, take a bad step. His boot slipped from an icy foothold, and he plunged downward.

Falling.

HEART OF THE LAND

ROLLAN HEARD ABEKE SCREAM AND AN ANGUISHED CRY from Meilin. Terror slammed into him—*I'm falling, I'm going to die*—when suddenly he wasn't falling. He was choking, and banging hard against the bumpy gray face of the cliff.

Something had him around his neck. Reaching up, he snagged taut cloth with his hand. Hoisting himself up, he eased the pressure on his throat. His feet found a tiny crack of rock to stand on, and, gasping for breath, he pressed himself against the rock face. Eyes closed, just breathing, Rollan clung to the cloth, his heart beating so hard that it felt like his whole body was shaking.

"Are you all right?" he heard Conor call from above him.

Without opening his eyes, he nodded. His throat felt bruised, and his shoulder was scraped from where he had slammed into the rock. His fingers were numb, but they clung like claws to the fabric that had stopped his fall.

Opening his eyes, he saw what it was.

Tarik's cloak, just beneath the brown layer, was now torn along the edge.

It had snagged a corner of rock, saving him.

Rollan released a shaky breath. "Thank you, Tarik," he whispered as the wind howled around him and the icy raindrops pricked like needles on his skin.

And . . . thank you, Worthy, for handing him the cloak earlier.

Looking up, he saw that his friends were waiting for him. "Keep going!" he shouted at them, his voice hoarse. He saw Meilin nod and lead the way.

Trying to steady his shaking hands, he made certain his green cloak was still covered beneath the brown one, and followed. *Don't look down*, he'd told Conor. He took his own advice, focusing on each handhold, the stone gritty and cold under his fingers, streaming with icy water. At last he looked up and saw Meilin at the edge of the cliff, helping Conor over and then reaching down to him. As he stretched to take her hand, the storm gave one last roar of thunder, and the wind yanked him away from the cliff face.

But Meilin held on tightly and dragged him over the edge of the cliff and onto the top of the island.

Rollan flopped over and lay there for a second, his eyes closed, feeling the last of the rain patter on his bare face. The stone was bumpy and hard against his back. And solid. He'd come closer than he ever had before to dying. Climbing down the cliff was going to be . . .

Well, he didn't want to think about it. Shivering, he opened his eyes and sat up. The other three were sitting, Abeke with her head on her knees, Conor looking out toward the horizon, where the storm was walking away on legs of lightning.

"Looking for the wave that you dreamed about?" Rollan croaked. He rubbed his throat, which was still sore. *I'll have bruises there*, he thought.

Brushing his wet hair out of his eyes, Conor shook his head. "I'm pretty sure this isn't the place."

"Completely sure would be better," Rollan said. Buffeted by the last of the wind, he got to his feet and surveyed the top of the island. As he'd seen through Essix's eyes, it was roughly square, and strangely flat, as if human hands had smoothed it. In its center was a weathered black rock about as high as his head, curved in the shape of a crescent. It seemed oddly familiar. Something about its shape . . .

Meilin stepped up next to him. "It's got the same surface as the gift," she said, reaching into her pocket. Carefully she pulled out the cloth-covered rock and unwrapped it. Conor and Abeke came to look at it, too.

And yes, Meilin was right. The huge, crescent-shaped rock in the center of the island was covered with obsidian-like black scales, just like the Heart of the Land stone.

"So now we reveal it," Rollan said. Followed by the others, he headed for the big rock, studying it, trying to figure out why it looked so familiar. In the middle it stood about head height, and it tapered down as it curved on each side to about a foot off the ground. He stepped into the center of the crescent; Meilin stood close beside him, and Abeke and Conor just behind. It was almost like being inside a circle, enclosed by the stone. It was quiet there, a kind of stillness that went beyond protection from the last of the storm's winds. It felt *old*, Rollan thought. Nobody had stood in this place for a long, long time.

"I think it's important that we're all here together," Abeke said softly from behind him.

Rollan nodded. She was right. Without each other's help, none of them would have made it to the top of the island.

Feeling almost reverent, Rollan laid a hand on the surface of the rock. It felt smooth under his fingers. Each scale was rounded, like a bump. Now that he was close to it, he could see that it wasn't entirely black; some of the bumps were a lighter color, almost orange, in a strange, mottled pattern.

"There," whispered Meilin, pointing.

Rollan looked and saw a hole in the huge stone, right at chest height, big enough to put his hand into. Immediately he understood. That is where they would reveal the Heart of the Land.

Meilin held out the rock. "You're from Amaya," she said to Rollan. "You should reveal it." Conor and Abeke nodded, agreeing.

Rollan felt goose bumps creep over his skin, and it wasn't because his clothes were sopping wet from the climb up the island. He looked around at his friends' faces, all as serious as he knew his was. "All right, I'll do it," he said. In the enclosed space, his voice echoed strangely.

Solemnly, he took the rock. It was heavier than it looked, and almost seemed to pulse with warmth. Turning to the huge stone that surrounded them, he gripped the rock in his fist and put his whole hand into the hole. It was like a tube, with a niche at the end. He pushed the stone into it. There was a click, the sound of a key turning in a lock. Quickly Rollan pulled his hand out.

A faint trembling arose from the stone at their feet. He and the others stared at each other. The mottled pattern on the huge stone that surrounded them became clearer, orange scales among the black.

Rollan examined it. He *knew* this pattern. At the same time, he finally realized why the shape of the rock had seemed so familiar. One end of the crescent had been roughly carved into the shape of a head with a wide, lizardlike mouth; the body of the lizard sculpture curved around them, ending in a stubby tail.

"A gila monster," he breathed. He'd seen gila monsters before. They were lizards of Amaya, desert reptiles that moved slowly over the stones that baked in the summer heat. But most were much smaller than this carved monolith.

Rollan had heard the legends of the great gila monster, of course. Every region of Erdas had its own myths, stories of powerful animals and their human partners. Typically they roamed around, rescuing maidens or princes and granting wishes and some such nonsense.

Zerif had once hoped to bank on those stories by bonding four young Conquerers to imposter legends, in order to discredit the newly reborn Four Fallen. Devin Trunswick, now Worthy, had been one of those very Conquerors.

"Rollan," whispered Abeke, her eyes wide. "Was this carving made to honor the *real* gila monster?"

As she spoke, there was a distant sound, like one huge rock scraping over another, and the trembling of the stone floor turned to shaking. A faint mist arose from the ground, filling the area inside the crescent. Then the mist started spinning slowly, becoming thicker.

To Rollan's astonishment, as the mist swirled around, it drew into itself into the shape of a woman standing in the center of the round room made by the curve of the gila monster's body. Her outlines were hazy, but he could see that she had a broad face with high cheekbones, a short, stocky, broad-shouldered body, and hair in two braids that hung down almost to her waist.

She was a woman long dead. She, Rollan felt sure, must have been the human partner to that legendary gila monster.

When the spirit spoke, Rollan heard it inside his head, not with his ears—a hollow, echoing rumble.

The lands of Erdas are facing their greatest threat, the spirit grated out, *and they send children. Children!* Her misty eyes seemed to look them over. *Eura. Nilo. Zhong.* Seeing Rollan, she nodded. *And Amaya. I am Kikimi.*

Rollan felt deeply reverent. This spirit existed outside of time. She was a legend. He bowed. "Greetings, Kikimi."

Then he felt Meilin's elbow in his side. "Did she speak to you?" she whispered.

"You didn't hear her?" Rollan whispered back.

All three of the other Greencloaks shook their heads, wide-eyed.

Rollan turned back to the spirit. "Kikimi," he said carefully, "we've come to reveal the Heart of the Land."

With a sound that rumbled in Rollan's bones like an earthquake, Kikimi nodded. Her face took on more heavy solidity. She looked like an idol carved out of living rock. When she spoke again, her hollow voice grew deeper and more echoey inside Rollan's head. *There is a great force in nature—and in human nature—that wants everything to fall apart, to be torn until there are no countries and no families and no friendships, and there is nothing left but a vast wasteland. That is the way of distrust, disunity, division, darkness, and . . .* She paused, and Rollan felt the weight of centuries bearing down on him. *Death,* the spirit concluded.

"What's she saying?" Abeke whispered to him.

"Darkness, other d-words, death," Rollan answered. "Now be quiet. She's saying something else."

The other way is unity, Kikimi intoned. *Do you choose the way of life and warmth and hope?*

"Yes," said Rollan. He turned to his friends. "Say yes," he urged.

"Yes!" they all said together.

It is well, the spirit said. *The Heart of the Land has been revealed. Take it.*

Rollan turned and saw that a warm glow was emanating from the hole in the side of the gila monster structure. Carefully he put his hand in, and he felt the bumpy surface of the rock—and more. Grasping it with his fingers, he pulled it out. The others gathered closer to see. In his hand, the scales covering the rock started to crumble like a burned crust, and fell away to show the revealed Heart of the Land, which glowed softly, a rounded chunk of amber stone with something dark trapped in its center. It had been carved and smoothed into the shape of a gila monster, tightly curled, its stubby tail tucked under its chin. And it was set on a chain—an amulet.

Rollan could feel it pulsing with power and possibility.

The spirit of the hero nodded, as if she could read his mind. *Anyone wielding the Heart can be as the gila monster,* she said.

Rollan looked up at her. Kikimi's eyes were oddly piercing, as if she were looking at him from across many, many years. "Be as . . . how?" he asked.

It is called the Heart of the Land for a reason, Kikimi said. *It was our two hearts, made into one. Unified.* The spirit cast a mournful glance at the face of the lizard that surrounded them.

And it offers great power, but power can be misused. The spirit turned, as if she was looking past them, toward the shore of the lake. Then she turned back. *Others are seeking the Heart. They will try to take it from you.*

As she spoke, the ground started trembling again. Little rags of mist started tearing from Kikimi's shape and whirling away. Her image faded. *Beware!* her hollow voice said, echoing in Rollan's head as she disappeared. *The Heart will give great power to* whoever *wields it, even if they are not Marked. You must not let the Heart fall into wicked hands!*

And then every wisp of mist was gone.

Rollan looked away and saw the other three Greencloaks staring at him.

Then they looked down at the amulet in Rollan's palm. It still glowed softly with its own light. The pattern on the sculpture that surrounded them had faded. It was as if they had been in a room separate from the outer world; all of a sudden, sounds from outside penetrated the room, and a breeze curled around their feet. Rollan looked out to see the clouds breaking up and the surface of the lake glinting where it was touched by beams of sunlight.

And . . . something else.

Quickly Rollan stepped out of the embracing circle of the gila monster sculpture and called Essix from passive state. She flashed out, catching the wind with her wings and soaring from the top of the island. Closing his eyes, Rollan looked at what she saw.

Black-clad figures had gathered on the shore of the lake.

Anka and Worthy stood on the sand bridge that led to the island. They were fighting, but they were being driven back, step by step.

The Oathbound army had arrived.

THE HAMMER

"THEY'RE HERE," ROLLAN SAID, WITH A QUICK GLANCE at Meilin.

She nodded, immediately understanding. The Heart of the Land had been revealed, and now the Oathbound would try to take it, and then arrest the Greencloaks.

"Let's go!" Abeke said. She headed for the edge of the island, where they could start climbing to the beach, far below. Meilin and the others followed.

Conor went first, resolutely not looking down. Then Abeke, and then Rollan, who was busy putting the revealed Heart into his pocket, and then Meilin was sliding on her stomach over the edge of the cliff, feeling for the first foothold with her boot.

She felt the need to hurry making her nerves jangle, but every step had to be carefully considered. She could hear faint shouts from the Oathbound as they rallied on the lakeshore.

Battle was awaiting them. They would need every weapon at their disposal.

"Rollan!" she called over her shoulder. Glancing down, she saw him pause and look up at her, then nod to show that he was listening. "How can we use the amulet in the fight?"

Rollan started climbing down again, his gaze on the stone cliff two inches from his nose. "I'm not sure," he panted. His voice sounded hoarse. "Kikimi–the spirit–she said that the Heart can make the wielder *as the gila monster.* I think gila monsters have a venomous bite. But there are stories. . . ." He paused while climbing over a tricky spot. "Be careful here," he said. "The rock's a little slippery."

Carefully, Meilin continued. Climbing down was definitely harder than climbing up. At least they weren't doing it in the middle of a howling thunderstorm. "Stories about the gila monster?" she prompted.

"Myths, really," Rollan called up to her. "They're sacred to some of the people who live in the west of Amaya. The gila monsters are burrowers. But," he added, sounding doubtful, "I don't think they are very powerful. They're kind of slow, and they like to stay hidden. The Heart might not be able to help us much."

Well, then, they wouldn't count on any help from the Heart. They were on their own. Meilin tried to ignore the dread gathering in her chest. There were hundreds of Oathbound waiting for them on the lakeshore. They'd been in some tough fights before, but they'd *never* faced odds this terrible. What if the Oathbound army's orders were to kill them instead of arresting them? They might not get out of this alive.

Below her, Abeke had reached the pebbly beach; a moment later, Conor joined her and they both called forth their spirit animals. Uraza bounded from the passive state with a snarl. Briggan raised his head and howled out a challenge to the Oathbound on the lakeshore. Essix swooped lower as Rollan jumped down to the beach, his heavy brown cloak swirling behind him. The falcon settled on his shoulder, her wings half open, ready to launch herself into flight as soon as Rollan gave the word. Abeke was busy stringing her bow and unwrapping the piece of leather that had protected the arrows in her quiver from the rain.

Meilin jumped down beside them and called Jhi from passive state. The panda yawned and then settled on her haunches, as if waiting to see what was going to happen. The presence of Jhi made Meilin feel suddenly stronger and more steady.

From the direction of the lakeshore came the sounds of shouted orders. The Oathbound had seen them reach the base of the cliff. Halfway along the bridge of sand, Worthy was fighting alone to keep a line of Oathbound attackers from crossing to the island. Fortunately, because the sand bridge was so narrow, he only had to face one attacker at a time. He was so fiercely fast and lithe from his black panther traits that he didn't even need any weapons, just his retractable claws. Behind him crouched the faint outline that was Anka. Hiding, not fighting.

The man coming for Worthy had a long spear. Worthy leaped back to avoid a thrust, and as his feet hit the sand it quivered and turned to liquid. He started sinking. Meilin heard the Redcloak yowl as he sank up to his knees. It had turned to quicksand—just as Worthy had feared!

The army of Oathbound soldiers—over a hundred, Meilin guessed—were massed on the beach, ready to converge on the Greencloaks once they fought their way across the bridge and reached the lakeshore.

"We are in big trouble," Rollan said, pulling out his knife.

"Six against a hundred or more," Abeke added. Gripping her bow, she bounced on the balls of her feet, looking ready to leap into action. "And they've got at least three Marked warriors with them."

Rollan squinted, using his keen sight to scan the enemy. "Yep. Wikam the Just with his vulture, and the spider guy. And an Amayan . . ." He shook his head. "His animal is something that flies really, really fast. I can't get a good look at it."

Meilin stepped quickly to Rollan's side. "If we're captured, can you give Essix the Heart so she can escape with it?"

He jerked out a quick nod, then rubbed his throat as if it hurt.

"Listen," Meilin said. Unsheathing her sword, she glanced around at her friends and their spirit animals. "We don't have to defeat them. We just have to fight through and escape. All right?"

"We're ready," Conor said, resting a hand on Briggan's head. The wolf panted, eager for battle.

Rollan nodded, and Abeke gave a neat salute with her bow. "Ready!"

"For the Greencloaks!" Meilin shouted, her heart pounding. "Let's go!"

She led the way, racing over the sand bridge. By the time she passed Anka and reached Worthy, he was up to his waist in the quicksand, bleeding from a wound in his side but still fighting furiously. With one swift stroke of her sword she dealt with the spearman who'd been poking at Worthy. He tumbled, shrieking, into the icy lake water.

A blur of gold and black, and Uraza bounded past. Abeke fired an arrow as she leaped, followed closely by Briggan and Conor, whose ax whirled above his head.

Meilin yelled in the direction she'd last seen Anka. "Help them!"

As she moved, Anka revealed herself, sand colored. She nodded, looking grim and a little scared, then went after the other Greencloaks.

There was a ripple down the line of Oathbound on the sand bridge, as the attackers turned to defenders, and their warlike shouts turned to cries of fear.

Quickly sheathing her sword, Meilin found firm footing. Behind the mask, she could see Worthy's eyes, wide and frightened.

"I'm very glad to see you at this particular moment," he gasped.

Seizing his hands, Meilin pulled with all her strength. But he was stuck, sinking deeper into the sucking sand. Ahead, she could hear the sound of Uraza's snarls, and screams and splashes as Abeke and Conor, with Anka's help, battled their way through the line of Oathbound on the sand bridge. But there were still way too many Oathbound, led by Wikam, waiting for them on the shore.

Panting, Meilin kept pulling at Worthy's hands, but he was already up to his chest. "Stop struggling!" she yelled at him. "You're only making it worse!"

Then, from behind her came a deep roar—a quick glance over her shoulder showed Jhi, her heavy body starting to sink. The panda lurched, and the quicksand flowed over her paws.

"Oh *no*," Meilin panted. Releasing Worthy's hands— he yowled in terror—she turned to call Jhi back into passive state; the panda went with a mournful roll of her dark eyes.

To her dismay, Rollan wasn't coming to help. He stood at the beginning of the sand bridge, and his lips were moving as if he was talking to himself. His long knife was lowered.

"Rollan!" she yelled. They needed him to fight!

He nodded, looking distracted. "Coming!" he shouted, but he didn't move.

Behind her, Worthy was babbling. "I'm sorry I ever thought you were scary, Meilin, just get me out of here, it's—gah! I'm sinking! I promise I'll do anything you—"

Meilin turned back to face him. "Shut up, Worthy," she muttered. He was up to his armpits now, his chin raised, keeping his mouth above the waves that lapped over the sand bridge. Grabbing his hands, she pulled.

Then, to her horror, the sand under her feet suddenly turned to liquid and she started to sink. In a blink, she was ankle deep in the sand. She tried to pull one foot out, and the other sank deeper.

"We are so *dooooomed*," she heard Worthy moan.

A second later, and she was trapped up to her knees. Twisting her body, she saw that Rollan had finally stepped onto the sand bridge. He looked like he was coming to help.

"Stay there!" she yelled frantically. "If you try to help us, you'll get trapped, too!"

But he kept coming, striding over the quivering sand. As he came, he raised his fist—he was holding the Heart amulet, and its amber glow leaked between his fingers.

Meilin felt a grinding thunder rumbling up from below. All around, the lake's waves churned, white with foam.

"Hold on!" Rollan shouted at her. Taking another step, he brought the hand holding the Heart down like a hammer. A deep boom rolled out from it, and with a whoosh, the quicksand holding Meilin and Worthy spat them out like a couple of melon seeds. Meilin stumbled to her knees, panting. Worthy lay on his stomach, trembling. "Ground," he mumbled, talking to the sand bridge, "if my arms were long enough, I would hug you right now." He got shakily to his feet. Blood was streaming from a cut over his ribs.

Without stopping, Rollan strode past them. "Get down!" he shouted to Abeke and Conor, and as they flattened themselves he brought the hammer down again. Meilin clung to the sand bridge as it writhed like a snake in an earthquake. Worthy wobbled and went to his knees behind her. All along the heaving bridge, the Oathbound were tossed into the lake, shrieking, throwing away their heavy weapons so they could swim.

Rollan whirled. Catching Meilin's eye, he grinned wildly, his hair tousled, his brown cloak whipping around him. "Heart of the *Land*, Meilin!" he shouted, and raised the glowing amulet in his clenched fist. "We should have realized—the gila monster has the power of the earth!"

22

BLOOD AND ARROWS

THE BRIDGE-QUAKE HAD KNOCKED ALL THE Oathbound into the lake. Abeke climbed to her feet, holding her bow well above the water so the string wouldn't get wet. Uraza bounded ahead of her. After a quick glance to see Conor and Briggan just a pace behind her, Abeke followed on light feet. Farther back was the blur that was Anka, and Meilin, her sword glinting in the light. Worthy was taking giant pantherlike leaps, his red cloak swirling behind him, and then came Rollan with Essix swooping low over his head, shrieking out a challenge.

Shaking back her braids, Abeke echoed that cry. "For the Greencloaks!" she shouted.

"For the Greencloaks!" her friends joined in.

"And the Redcloaks!" Worthy yowled.

Her teeth bared with excitement, Abeke looked ahead as she raced along the narrow bridge. On the shore awaited a wall of Oathbound soldiers, all dressed in black uniforms with brass armor protecting their necks and their lower arms. Farther back she saw Wikam the Just, taller than all the others, issuing orders. The huge vulture was hunched on his shoulder.

Wikam, who wanted to unjustly arrest the Green-cloaks, throw them into a prison, and condemn them to death—for something they hadn't done!

He would be her target.

Snarling, Uraza reached the shore first, and the Oathbound soldiers fell back before her, giving Abeke room to begin her attack. As the other Greencloaks swarmed off the sand bridge, Abeke and Uraza cut sideways, using their leopard-given stealthiness to dodge a spear thrust. Another leap, and Abeke was past two more Oathbound swordsmen, drawing an arrow from her quiver and trying to spot Wikam amid the whirl of fighting. Uraza crouched beside her, ready to pounce. From the lakeshore by the sand bridge came the sound of clashing weapons, shouted orders, and then Briggan's howl as he entered the fray.

Wikam was pointing out where his soldiers should strike next, surrounded by a personal guard of six burly warriors, all bearing sharp-pointed pikes that kept him clear of the battle. His vulture launched itself from his shoulder, flapping its wings to gain height.

Uraza snarled, keeping the attacking Oathbound at bay while Abeke drew back her bowstring, sighting down the arrow at her target.

At that very moment, Wikam turned, and they locked eyes across a mass of Oathbound who were charging into the fight.

You're mine, Abeke thought fiercely. She felt the rightness of the shot and released the arrow. It flashed across the space separating her from Wikam, flying straight and true toward his heart.

Abeke had time to feel a moment of exultation—*got you!*—when a huge, black-feathered shape swooped down and snatched the arrow out of the air just before it reached its target. The bird flapped upward, croaking in triumph, the arrow clutched in its bony talons. Wikam's vulture!

Immediately Abeke reached for another arrow, nocked it, and fired. Seeing it coming, Wikam grabbed one of his own soldiers, pulling the man in front of him. The arrow plunged into the man's chest. Blood spattered across Wikam's face. Almost carelessly, he tossed the man aside like a cracked shield. Abeke was ready with another arrow, but it was too late. The Oathbound guards had closed in around Wikam, making him impossible to reach.

She heard Wikam scream an order. A troop of ten Oathbound split off from the main battle. Bearing swords and spears, they advanced on Abeke. Uraza snarled, and ten *more* warriors came after her.

Backing away, Abeke trained an arrow on one, and then another of the Oathbound.

But she only had seven arrows left.

It wouldn't be enough.

BLOOD AND AX
BLADES

WHEN ABEKE AND URAZA WENT LEFT, CONOR AND
Briggan cut their way into the middle of Wikam's
fighters. Conor's wolflike strength and speed meant none
of the Oathbound could match him, and Briggan at his
back meant they couldn't attack him from behind.

With a yell, Conor whirled his ax over his head, clearing a space around himself and Briggan. One big
Oathbound warrior with a huge double-bladed ax stepped
over a wounded comrade, right into the opening. He had
braided both his fiery red hair and his long beard. The
man roared out a challenge. "Come to me, Greencloak!"
he shouted. "And learn how to die!" And with heavily
muscled arms, he strode forward, swinging the ax, trying
to chop Conor in half.

Conor felt the breeze of its passing as he ducked out
of the way.

With a frustrated shout, the warrior lifted the ax high
above his head and brought it down like an executioner,
aiming for Conor's neck. Conor leaped aside, and the ax
thudded into the stony ground.

Too close, Conor thought. The man was big, but he
was fast, too. Conor had to end this.

Another dodge and a roll, and Conor got inside the warrior's guard. Reversing his grip on his weapon, Conor smashed the butt of his ax under the warrior's bearded chin.

But the blow just seemed to make him angier. Roaring with pain and outrage, the warrior went berserk, his ax hacking wildly through the air.

Conor couldn't fight a madman. "Let's go!" he shouted to Briggan, and they retreated, pursued by five Oathbound and the bearded warrior.

BLOOD AND AMULET

ROLLAN SET FOOT ON THE LAKESHORE JUST AS WORTHY, yowling out a challenge, landed crouched in the middle of a group of Oathbound. They converged on him, and then there was a sort of explosion as Worthy turned into a snarling, whirling weapon of destruction. Screaming black-clad figures went flying in every direction.

Off to the side, Abeke was taking aim at something with her bow, and Meilin had drawn her sword while calling Jhi out of passive state. Conor was being chased by a pack of Oathbound, with Briggan protecting his back. Even Anka was using her new fighting skills to attack Oathbound seemingly out of nowhere.

In Rollan's hand, the Heart of the Land burned hot like stone that had been baking under a desert sun. Frantically, he racked his brain trying to remember the stories he'd heard about the legendary gila monster. The amulet was clearly powerful. If he could figure out how to use it, they might be able to defeat the Oathbound army.

Something green and black whizzed past his head, and he flinched away. An arrow?

No—it swooped around, chirping angrily, and darted back toward him. A hummingbird! Not too much of a threat, he thought. It was only a tiny bird. It was the spirit animal of the Marked Amayan Oathbound, who raced toward Rollan brandishing a rapier—a thin sword with a wickedly sharp point. Still holding up the Heart, Rollan ripped the long knife from his belt in time to block the Marked Oathbound's attack. The hummingbird flashed past his face again, distracting him, and he barely managed to evade the next thrust. He felt a thin line of pain along his cheekbone. Shaking his head, a few drops of blood flew out. Had the bird cut him? Then the Oathbound struck again, and the rapier slid past Rollan's ribs, ripping a hole in both of his cloaks. At the same moment, the hummingbird darted straight toward his face. It was aiming its sharp beak at his eyes—it was trying to blind him!

Seeing Rollan in trouble, Essix dove in, her talons reaching for the hummingbird, but it was too swift, easily evading her and flashing in for another attack.

Rollan threw up his arm to protect his eyes from the hummingbird's sharp beak.

Then something hit him hard from the side and he was slammed to the ground. As he landed, the Heart of the Land amulet popped out of his hand and went tumbling among the stones that littered the lakeshore. Rollan struggled against the heavy weight that had hit him—an Oathbound twice his size with hugely muscled arms.

Rollan slashed at her with his long knife, but the edge of the blade hit her brass collar. She responded by jerking him to his feet and wrapping one of her arms around his neck.

"Wikam's orders!" shouted the Oathbound to the Marked Amayan as Rollan struggled to breathe. His feet weren't even touching the ground! "Get the amulet!" she screamed.

The Marked Oathbound went to his knees, the hummingbird circling his head. To his dismay, Rollan saw him pick up the Heart—then came a blur of feathers, and Essix swooped down to snatch it from his fingers, soaring into the sky with the Heart clutched in her talons.

Rollan choked out a yell of triumph, and the Oathbound woman squeezed harder, cutting off his air. He'd already been choked once today—this was really too much! Black spots formed before his eyes, and he clawed at the burly arm that was wrapped around his throat. He was starting to see why wearing neck armor might be a good idea.

Then he heard a grunt and the pressure on his throat let up. As he went to his knees, gasping for breath, the Oathbound crashed to the ground beside him, unconscious. He looked up to see Anka fading into the background.

"Thanks!" Rollan rasped.

He saw what looked like a faint grin cross her face, and then she disappeared again.

He climbed to his feet, rubbing the new bruises on his neck, trying to spot Essix—and the Heart—but what he saw made his own heart sink.

Twenty feet away, Meilin had been separated from Jhi and was surrounded by Oathbound. She was a whirlwind of attacks, all efficiency and focus. Her movements were a blur—a chop at one Oathbound's neck, a blow aimed at another's ribs, followed by a precise strike at that particular place where boys really don't want to be hit.

But when that Oathbound fell at her feet, writhing in pain, another leaped forward to take his place. There were too many of them!

Worthy was surrounded, too. The Redcloak was bleeding from wounds on both arms, a leg, and his chest, and every time he whirled to rip at an Oathbound attacker with his claws, droplets of his own blood sprayed around him. His mask had been hacked in half, revealing one catlike eye and a snarling mouth. He was fierce, but his movements were slowing.

Conor was outnumbered, too, though he had used his ax and wolf-given speed to clear an area around him. Abeke had run out of arrows and was using her bow as a staff as she fought an Oathbound armed with a spear.

"Essix!" Rollan shouted desperately, searching the sky. Then he glimpsed the falcon from the corner of his eye. With Wikam's vulture on her tail, she dove toward him, holding the Heart in her talons. Rollan reached to meet her, and his fingers closed around the amulet. The vulture, a moment behind, raked its claws across Rollan's hand, trying to get him to drop the stone, but he held on, ignoring the flash of pain over his knuckles.

The vulture gave a guttural hiss and banked awkwardly, coming around for another attack.

As Rollan ducked, he saw that Wikam had ordered another group of Oathbound to form up for an attack—at least twenty of them. Worthy and Meilin would be overwhelmed; Conor and Abeke would not be able to help.

Rollan slashed at the diving vulture with his long knife and then tried the same move that had cleared the Oathbound from the sand bridge, bringing down his hand holding the Heart like a hammer. Thunder rolled out, and under the Heart's power the land bucked and heaved. The attacking Oathbound were flung onto their knees. But so were his friends. As the earthquake passed, they all jumped to their feet again, picked up the weapons they'd dropped, and the fight resumed.

"All right, that didn't work," Rollan muttered to himself. "Gila monster." He backed away as two Oathbound came at him with swords drawn. "Lizard," he chanted frantically. "Uh . . . burrows in the ground." He gripped the Heart. "Burrower!" he shouted.

The group of Oathbound had almost reached the spot where Meilin and Worthy were now fighting back-to-back.

Swooping forward with the speed of one of Essix's dives, Rollan punched the fist holding the amulet toward the Oathbound attackers. He felt power roll out, and with a rumble and a heave of dirt, a sinkhole opened right under the Oathbounds' feet. All twenty of them tumbled down, shrieking. Their cries grew louder as Rollan gestured again and the dirt flowed back, covering them up to their necks.

"Hah!" he yelled.

Worthy echoed him, yowling with glee.

Meilin connected a blow with an opponent's head and then spun around, checking for attackers, but she'd dealt with all of them. Rollan's eyes met hers; she gave a nod of approval.

And then she looked past him, and her eyes went wide with dismay.

Whirling, Rollan saw what she was looking at.

Wikam had been holding even more Oathbound in reserve. A large group of archers aimed their powerful longbows. They had nocked their heavy arrows, tipped with razor-sharp barbs. At Wikam's shouted command, the archers drew back their bowstrings.

Rollan's heart froze. The Oathbound leader was not trying to capture them anymore. This wasn't about justice. His archers were aiming to kill.

"Get down!" Rollan heard Abeke scream.

But it was too late.

The archers fired. A storm of arrows streaked through the air.

Aimed at the Greencloaks' hearts.

25

REDCLOAKS

As the Oathbound archers released their arrows, Meilin knew she was about to die. She and her best friends would be struck by enough arrows to kill them instantly. Instinctively, she looked for Rollan, expecting to see his face pale with fright as he faced death.

But instead, his eyes were bright as he held up the glowing Heart of the Land. "Gila monster!" he was shouting. "Armor!"

The arrows, black and deadly, hissed through the air. They were mere inches away as Rollan's hand went out in a blocking gesture, and every single arrow suddenly stopped, hung in the air for a second, and then fell to the ground with a clatter.

"Rollan, I think I love you . . . " was Worthy's breathless comment.

"Ooh, arrows!" Abeke exclaimed. She started gathering them up, stuffing as many as she could into her quiver.

"Another gila monster trait," Rollan said, grinning. "They're associated with armor. The other one that I can think of is their venomous bite." He cocked his head. "Think I can get close enough to Wikam to bite him?"

Meilin glanced in that direction. Her heart dropped. "No," she said briefly, and raised her sword, ready to fight. Behind her, Jhi gave a mournful roar.

The Oathbound archers had set down their bows and had drawn swords. A shrieked order from Wikam, and they charged toward the five Greencloaks and Worthy.

"Time for another sinkhole!" Rollan said, raising the Heart of the Land.

But the Oathbound were ready for that.

As Rollan punched his fist, holding the Heart toward the mass of fighters, they parted, racing around the sinkhole that opened in the ground. Another wave of attackers followed.

A moment later, Meilin and her allies were surrounded by a thicket of gleaming swords.

"Surrender!" screamed Wikam, who had followed his fighters. They were opening up a way for him to get to the Greencloaks. His vulture swooped low, then landed on his shoulder, its ugly face looking smug with victory.

Meilin saw Worthy's shoulders slump, and Abeke lowered her bow. A glance at Rollan, and he shook his head, eyes wide. The Heart couldn't save them now.

"There's nothing I can do," Anka said from beside her. "I can't hide us when we're right in front of them."

"Throw down your weapons, renegade Greencloaks," Wikam ordered, "and put your spirit animals into passive state!"

Meilin saw Rollan glance up, looking for Essix—she could escape with the Heart.

"If I see that falcon come near the amulet," Wikam shouted, "I will have it shot from the air!"

Rollan gulped and lowered his fist. The Heart of the Land's glow was fading.

Slowly, Meilin straightened. The excitement of battle drained from her muscles, leaving her shaking. It was over. They couldn't resist without being killed. She called Jhi, and the panda went into the passive state; Abeke and Conor had done the same with Uraza and Briggan. Essix was nowhere to be seen.

"Lay down your weapons!" Wikam ordered. Tall and gaunt, he stood with arms crossed, just behind the first row of Oathbound fighters, who still had their swords drawn. "It is time for you to face the justice you deserve."

Meilin knew that justice was exactly what they *wouldn't* get from Wikam.

All he would offer them was death.

Conor was bending to set his ax on the ground when suddenly Worthy ripped off the remains of his mask and let out a sound that was part snarl, part yowl, and fiercely triumphant. *"Redcloaks!"* he shouted. "To me!"

Meilin stared in astonishment as a group of twelve red-cloaked, mask-wearing fighters burst from the forest near the lake and raced across the pebbly shoreline toward them.

Seeing the new threat, Wikam whirled and started shrieking orders to his Oathbound. Half stayed to guard the Greencloaks; the other half, at least forty fighters, split off to meet the newcomers.

The Redcloaks were outnumbered three to one, but each of them had the power, speed, and strength of the spirit animals they were once bonded with. It was an even fight . . . almost.

"Now is our chance to escape!" Worthy shouted.

Meilin nodded; the others were already raising their weapons again. She saw Worthy exchange a kind of salute with the leader of the Redcloaks—who wore a white mask in the shape of a ram's face.

Worthy, she realized, had *known* the Redcloak fighters had been coming to help them!

No sense in wasting this opportunity.

"Let's go!" Meilin shouted, and with a lightning-fast move, she disarmed the nearest Oathbound fighter, seizing her sword for herself. A sweeping strike with that sword, and she was through the line of guards; the others followed. In the distance she heard a howl of outrage as Wikam realized the Greencloaks were getting away. A group of Oathbound broke off from those fighting the Redcloaks and started in pursuit. The Redcloaks, using their superhuman speed, raced to block them.

"Shouldn't we help?" Abeke called, looking back over her shoulder. She had one of the Oathbound arrows in her hand and looked ready to nock it and let it fly.

"Stead and the others are giving us time to escape!" Worthy panted. He pointed toward the forest path.

"Wait!" Rollan shouted, and stumbled to a halt. The others gathered around him, panting. "They'll know exactly where we've gone, and we can't outrun them for long. The vulture will track us."

Down the beach, the Redcloaks were fighting wildly, holding back the mass of black-clad Oathbound.

"We have to go!" Worthy yowled frantically.

"We'd better run," Meilin agreed.

"No," Rollan said briefly. "I just realized what it means that gila monsters are burrowers." He raised his hand—

still holding the Heart of the Land. It glowed brightly again. "Tunnel!" he shouted.

With a rumble, the pebbles at their feet shifted; they all jumped back as a hole in the ground opened, just big enough to crawl into.

Rollan bent to peer into it. "It's a tunnel, all right." Crumbles of dirt fell from around the opening. It didn't look very stable.

"You go first," Worthy said, looking doubtful.

Rolling his eyes, Rollan crawled in. His voice drifted back to them. "It's opening up ahead of me. It's leading away! Come on!"

One by one, they followed, keeping their spirit animals in passive state. Meilin went last. As she crawled into the hole, following Worthy, the dirt caved in behind her. She felt a moment of panic—they'd be trapped!—when she realized that the tunnel was closing behind them, hiding where they had gone.

She crawled for what seemed like a long, long time in utter blackness.

"I hate this," she heard Worthy mutter.

She didn't like it much, either, but there was no way the Oathbound could track them underground. This was their best chance to escape.

"It's really dark in here," came Worthy's complaining voice. Then Meilin heard him mutter, *"Shut up, Worthy."*

She had been about to say the same thing. Instead she reached forward in the dark until she felt Worthy's ankle. She gave it a reassuring pat. "It's all right," she said softly. "We're all scared."

"Even you?" he whispered.

"Even me," she said.

"Oh," she heard him say. And then, even more quietly, "Thanks, Meilin."

Her knees were starting to get sore, and she knew she was covered with dirt. She had dirt in her hair and under her fingernails. She really hated being dirty.

Something long and soft—a furry rope?—brushed her face, and she flinched back. The tunnel fell in behind her, forcing her to go on.

The furry rope touched her cheek again, and she reached up quickly, grabbed it, and pulled hard.

"Owww!" Worthy yowled, from just ahead of her.

Quickly she let go of the furry rope. Wait. Was it a—? Did Worthy have a—?

There was a sudden muffled shout from ahead, and a burst of light blinded her.

26

WORTHY

WITH A HEAVE, THE GROUND SPAT THEM ALL OUT. ALL six of them—the four Greencloak kids, Anka, and Worthy—lay on the forest floor, panting. The tunnel had disappeared. There was no sound of fighting. There was no path.

Worthy knew he should get up, but he felt so comfortable, just lying there. Above, pine branches swayed quietly in a light breeze. So peaceful. His eyes dropped closed.

Around him, the others were sitting up.

"I think we're clear," he heard Meilin's voice say.

"I'll ask Uraza to check our tail," Abeke said. "Our trail, I mean."

Worthy heard other sounds, and then he felt prickly, as if he was being watched. He opened his eyes to see Meilin standing at his feet, looking down at him. The panda loomed behind her.

Nearby stood Abeke, holding her bow, and Rollan, with Essix on his shoulder. Next to them was Conor, Briggan panting at his side. Anka was there, too, a blur of forest green.

For some reason the four Greencloaks and Anka were all smiling at him.

Worthy sat up, then climbed wearily to his feet. He was so tired—even his bones hurt. He glanced down at his arm.

There was a slash in his sleeve. A wound! "Gah!" he exclaimed. "Blood!" There was blood on his pants, too, and on his shirt. A second later, he felt the pain from four different wounds hit him at once.

With a yowl, he flopped back onto the ground. "I'm dying!" he moaned. "Farewell. Think kindly of me when I'm gone."

Meilin crouched beside him. "Worthy."

He gazed pitifully up at her. "What?" he said weakly.

"These are flesh wounds," Meilin said.

He blinked. "So I'm not dying?"

"No, you're not dying." He started to sit up, but she put a gentle hand on his shoulder and held him down. "You are hurt, though. Stay there."

"What you need," Rollan said, "is some panda spit."

"Yes," Meilin agreed. "Jhi can help."

Worthy lay still as the big panda lumbered over to him. Her pink tongue licked the slash on his arm, then the cut over his ribs, and then the two other wounds. A feeling of peace settled over him. The stinging pain from his injuries faded away. "Panda spit," he murmured. "I see what you mean."

Now he really didn't feel like getting up.

"Just rest," he heard Meilin say.

No problem. Worthy lay there listening to the Greencloaks tell Anka what had happened up on the Heart of the Land island while he and the chameleon woman had fought together on the sand bridge.

Something about a spirit and a warning, and a gila monster.

"It's quite a ... um ... tale," he heard Rollan say.

Wearily, Worthy let their words wash over him. In a minute he would tell them what he knew about the second gift to the Greencloaks. Or, rather, what he'd guessed. His own family had once possessed an ancestral sword. It had been modeled after a famous sword from Euran history.

Something about a claw.

Eurans had always told stories about a legendary black wildcat. Long ago, such a wildcat had roamed the country with his human partner. The tales told of a great sword that the two used to defend their home.

The Wildcat's Claw.

This gift probably had great powers, just like the Heart of the Land, but it had been hidden, too. And nobody knew exactly what its powers had been.

Devin Trunswick's family sword had just been a replica of that great sword, but if there was a record of the real gift, it was likely somewhere in Trunswick.

He, Worthy, would lead them to it.

The Greencloaks were still talking.

"You know," Conor was saying, "Princess Song was on our side before. I think we should try getting a message to her."

"Telling her what?" Worthy heard Meilin ask.

"We might be able to convince her about the Fakecloaks," Conor answered.

Typical, Worthy thought to himself. Conor always thought the best of people. He wondered if Conor thought the best of *him* now. Had he proven himself enough? Would the Greencloaks let him stay with them?

"No," he heard Anka say. "We can't risk contacting anyone. We have to keep going. We have to find the other gifts."

"And we don't even know where to start," Meilin said.

Worthy smiled, knowing they would trust him even more, once he'd helped them with that. "So . . ." he interrupted, opening his eyes. "Was I a hero? During the fight with the Oathbound?"

The five of them broke off their conversation and glanced over at him.

He sat up.

Did the Greencloaks approve of him? Did they truly accept him? He knew his expression was giving away how desperately he hoped they did, so he groped in the pocket of his cloak for the extra mask that every Redcloak carried at all times. Carefully, he tied it over his face, concealing his features.

But he couldn't conceal what he knew, not any longer. "We'll have to look for the sword next. The Wildcat's Claw, wielded by a legendary hero of Eura." He gulped. "When I . . . when I went over to the Conquerors, I let Zerif bond me to the black panther." He looked up, meeting Conor's eyes. "I'm really, *really* sorry about that. I wanted . . ." He shrugged. "I wanted to be a hero."

All four of the Greencloaks looked down at him. Meilin's eyebrows were raised. A corner of Rollan's mouth quirked up.

"You definitely were a hero in the battle against the Oathbound," Conor answered at last. Even Briggan looked like he was smiling.

"We are very glad to have you with us," Abeke added.

Worthy let their approval sink in for a moment. Then, with a weary sigh, he climbed stiffly to his feet.

They were all grinning widely at him.

He smiled back at them. He really was part of the team. He'd never been happier. Then, to his horror, he felt his long, furry secret uncurl from behind his red cloak.

Rollan gave a shout of laughter.

Oh *no*! Worthy buried his masked face in his hands.

"Wait, what?" he heard Anka's sharp voice exclaim. "Worthy has a *tail*?"

Sarah Prineas is the author of The Magic Thief, Winterling, and Ash & Bramble series. She lives in Iowa with her mad-scientist husband, two kids, two dogs, two cats, chickens, and a bunch of goats.

BOOK SIX

THE WILDCAT'S CLAW

Now fugitives, the young heroes must clear their names while evading the ruthless Oathbound. Together, they head for the familiar town of Trunswick, seeking a legendary sword. But they find the city transformed: the castle burned to the ground and the townsfolk poor and desperate.

With a handsome reward being offered for their capture, who can the heroes trust?